D1187060

The Wonderful Worlds
of
WALT DISNEY

FANTASYLAND

Illustrations by The Walt Disney Studio

GOLDEN PRESS · NEW YORK

CONTENTS

Library of Congress Catalog Card Number: 65-26170
© Copyright 1965 by Walt Disney Productions. All rights reserved. Stories and pictures in this book previously copyrighted © 1961, 1958, 1957, 1955, 1953, 1952, 1951, 1950, 1949, 1948, 1947, 1946, 1940, 1938, 1934, 1933 by Walt Disney Productions. Designed, produced, and published by Golden Press, New York, a division of Western Publishing Company, Inc. Printed in the U.S.A.

BONGO is based on the original story "Bongo" copyright 1930 by Hearst Magazines, Inc., successors to International Magazine Co., Inc.

DUMBO OF THE CIRCUS was suggested by the story "Dumbo, the Flying Elephant" by Helen Aberson and Harold Pearl, copyright 1939 by Roll-A-Book Publishers, Inc.

FOREWORD

Over the years we have had the privilege of adapting for the screen the works of some of the finest story-tellers the world has ever known—the Brothers Grimm, Aesop, Hans Christian Andersen and Perrault, right up to P. L. Travers, author of "Mary Poppins." We are most appreciative that our films have been received warmly both by the public and the critics.

For most of this time—over forty years, in fact—we have been transferring our film stories to the printed page in books for all the family. These offerings have covered a wide spectrum of publishing—the classics, modern versions of ancient tales, our own adventures of Mickey Mouse and Donald Duck, and a wealth of new fables whose heroes are the creatures of woodland, prairie, and desert.

The relationship with our publishers has been a close and happy one, and now the fruits of this collaboration are presented in this set of four books for the entire family. We hope you will enjoy them.

WALT DISNEY

THE SLEEPING BEAUTY

ONCE UPON A TIME in a land far away, there lived a handsome king and his fair queen. Their land was at peace and they had many friends. The king and queen should have been perfectly happy in their great castle on the hill.

But, alas, they were not because they had no child. For many years to have a child had been their dearest wish. Then, at last, the wish was granted. A baby daughter was born to them. And so lovely was she, so sweet and full of promise, that they called her Aurora, which means The Dawn.

The day of Aurora's christening was a holiday throughout the kingdom. And everyone, both high and low, was invited to pay homage to the infant princess. It was a day of great joy and celebration.

The streets of the royal city were crowded that morning with happy country folk. They were bringing to the castle their finest fruit, their fattest and fleeciest flocks, and their loyal hearts as offerings.

There were knights in armor on the roads that day, and soldiers in coats of mail, and lovely ladies. All had come to toast the King and his lovely Queen—and especially small Princess Aurora. The castle was gay with banners and flags and the courtyard was swarming with happy people. But the happiest of all were those in the throne room, close to the cradle of the royal child. They were good King Stefan and his Queen.

The King and Queen welcomed their royal guests—King Hubert of the neighboring kingdom and Prince Phillip, his small son. It had long been the dream of both friendly kings that one day their small kingdoms should be joined.

To do this Prince Phillip and little Princess Aurora would be betrothed. And when the princess came of age, the two of them would be wed.

Prince Phillip had brought a gift for the Princess. He felt quite grown-up when he presented it to the Queen.

Then he stepped to the cradle for a look at the small princess. Now babies did not interest Prince Phillip much. But at that moment his eye was caught by something that *did* interest him.

Three tiny, bright creatures floated down a beam of sunlight. They were the three good fairies—Mistress Flora, Mistress Fauna, and Mistress Merryweather. They too had come to present their gifts to the Princess.

Flora spoke first. "Little Princess," she said, "my gift shall be the gift of rare beauty." A shower of sunbeams shimmered down into the cradle.

Next Fauna said, "My gift is song your whole life long." Flower petals floated down upon the cradle.

Then Merryweather began, "Sweet Princess, my gift to you shall be—"

But before she could say any more, the wicked fairy Maleficent appeared.

"To show you that I bear no ill will for not being invited," Maleficent said, "I too shall bestow a gift on the child. Before the sun sets on her sixteenth birthday, the Princess shall prick her finger on the spindle of a spinning wheel—and die!"

"Oh, no!" gasped the Queen.

"Seize her!" cried the King.

But Maleficent disappeared in a bolt of lightning.

Then Merryweather spoke. "I cannot undo the curse, but I still have my wish. Sweet Princess, if you should prick your finger, you shall not die. You shall lie in a magic sleep and wake when true love's kiss shall break the spell."

"Burn every spinning wheel!" King Hubert said to King Stefan. "If there aren't any in the kingdom, the Princess can't prick her finger."

As night fell on Princess Aurora's christening day, the dusk was brightened with a fiery glow. In every town a great fire was kindled. And before those fires died, every spinning wheel in the kingdom had been burned.

In the deserted throne room the three fairies sat.

"Even a bonfire won't stop Maleficent," said Merryweather sadly.

"There must be some way," Flora muttered. "Walls may have ears," she said. "Follow me."

Flora swiftly turned herself into a tiny light and twinkled up to a jeweled box. The others followed her. Then they all settled down for a talk where even Maleficent couldn't overhear them.

"There's just one thing Maleficent won't expect," said Flora. "There's one thing she doesn't understand. And that is love."

Her voice dropped to an excited whisper. "Of course, we'll have to plan it carefully— Let's see, there's the woodcutter's cottage, the abandoned one. The King and Queen will object, but when we explain it's the only way—"

"Explain what?" asked Merryweather. "What are you talking about?"

"About the three peasant women raising a foundling child, deep in the forest."

"That's very nice of them," said Fauna. "Who are they?"

Flora waved her wand. Fauna and Merryweather looked at themselves in surprise. They were the peasant women!

"You mean," gasped Merryweather, "it's us?"

"Why not?" said Flora. "We'll take care of the baby."

"I'd like that!" said Merryweather. "And we'll have our magic, of course."

"No," said Flora sternly. "No magic!" And before they could protest, she snatched away their wands.

"You mean, live like mortals for sixteen years?" gasped Merryweather. "We've never done anything without magic. Who'll wash and cook and—?"

"Oh, we'll all pitch in," said Flora. "And that's why Maleficent won't suspect us."

"Well," said Merryweather and Fauna.

"Come," said Flora, "we must tell their majesties at once."

And off they went to the King and Queen, because it did indeed seem the best way to guard the baby princess from harm. The King and Queen agreed.

Good King Stefan and his beloved Queen watched with heavy hearts that night as the fairies and their daughter disappeared into the night.

clustered at a table, busy with a thick book of dress patterns.

"I pick this one," said Flora, putting her finger on a picture of a beautiful gown.

"Oh, she'll look beautiful in that," sighed Fauna.

"But how are we going to get her out of the house?" Merryweather, the practical one, said. "We can't surprise her if she's here."

Just then Briar Rose came down the stairs. They didn't see her until she spoke. "Well, what are you three dears up to?"

"Up to?" the aunts repeated.

"Why, my dear," said Merryweather hastily, "we want you to pick some berries."

"That's it," said the others, "lots of berries." And handing her a basket and her scarf, they all but pushed Briar Rose out the door.

So off into the woods went Briar Rose. And the aunts called after her:

"Don't hurry back!"

"But don't go too far!"

"And don't talk to strangers!"

"Good-bye, Good-bye, Good-bye!"

"I'll get the wands," said Merryweather, as soon as Briar Rose had gone.

"No wands," said Flora, "we're taking no chances."

"But I've never baked a cake," said poor Merryweather.

"You won't have to," said Fauna. "I'm going to bake the cake. I'm going to make it fifteen layers high, with pink and blue forget-me-nots, and candles."

"And I'm going to make the dress," said Flora.

Before Merryweather could ask a question, Flora flipped a length of cloth over her head. She slashed a hole at the bottom and a hole at the top, and holes in both sides, for sleeves.

"How does it look?" Flora asked her.

"It looks awful," said Merryweather crossly. "I still say we ought to use magic."

The years passed, as the years do, and for King Stefan and his Queen, they were lonely, anxious years.

But it was not so at the woodcutter's cottage, deep in the forest. Indeed, the little hut often rang with songs and merry laughter. For in that cottage the baby princess was growing into the loveliest of maidens . . . And what was her name? Well, the three aunts who had raised her with loving care called her Briar Rose.

At last it was almost the day of Briar Rose's birthday. What a flurry there was in the woodcutter's cottage! Briar Rose's three aunts, Flora, Fauna, and Merryweather, were

"But it's a lovely shade of pink," said Flora.

Merryweather said, "I wanted it blue."

Pink or blue, the dress did look awful. And it seemed likely that the cake would turn out worse.

Fauna tried to follow the recipe. But she didn't know that eggs had to be broken, and the layers of batter ran together in a mess.

"Enough of this nonsense," Merryweather snapped. "I'm going to get the wands."

And when she stamped up the stairs, with Flora's dress falling to pieces around her at each step, neither of the others could disagree.

While the fairies were having such a time at home, Briar Rose was spending a lonely day in the deep woods.

Because she had been protected all her life, the only friends Briar Rose had were the woodland animals and birds. As soon as she sat down on a fallen tree trunk, they surrounded her. The sleepy rabbits woke up from their naps and the saucy squirrels came running.

But today it was a bit sad. Suddenly the woodland friends were not quite enough any more.

"Oh dear!" Briar Rose said. "Why do they still treat me like a child?"

"Whooo?" asked the owl.

"Aunt Flora and Fauna and Merryweather," said Briar Rose. "And I so much want to meet someone."

"Whooo?" asked the owl.

"Oh," said Briar Rose, "someone tall and handsome and romantic. We'd walk together and talk together—well, it's only a dream." And because it was only a dream, Briar Rose sadly hid her face in her hands.

Now it happened that on that very day the Prince of the neighboring country, Phillip by name, was riding alone through the woods. Suddenly he stopped, for he thought he heard a beautiful song.

It was Briar Rose he heard. She could not stay sad for long and was singing.

"Do you hear that, Samson?" Phillip said to his horse. "Come on, let's find out who it is."

As the Prince came up behind Briar Rose on the woodland path, he thought she was the loveliest thing he had ever seen.

"I know you," Briar Rose sang to Phillip. "I walked with you once upon a dream."

"I know you," the Prince sang with her. He caught Briar Rose in his arms and they danced down the path.

"Oh!" said Briar Rose, pulling free. "I forgot, you're a—a—"

"A stranger?" asked the Prince.

"Yes," said Briar Rose.

"But we've met before. Don't you remember? You said so yourself," the Prince said, "once upon a dream."

"Oh!" said Briar Rose, and she let the Prince take her hand in his. Together they walked down the woodland path singing their song.

"Who are you?" the Prince asked. "What is your name?"

"My name is—oh, no, I mustn't," cried Briar Rose, remembering her aunts' warnings. "Good-bye!"

And away she ran, toward home.

"When will I see you?" the Prince called.

"Never, oh, never, never!" Briar Rose called back sadly.

"When?" the Prince asked again. "Tomorrow?"

He seemed terribly sad, and that was too much for Briar Rose to bear. She wanted him to be happy.

"Not tomorrow," Briar Rose said, because suddenly it seemed so far away. "This evening—at the woodcutter's cottage in the woods."

13

Back at the cottage, preparations for the surprise party were going on more smoothly, with the help of the fairies' magic wands.

Flour, eggs and milk mixed together and made a lovely cake. Needle flashed up and down and sewed a beautiful ball gown.

As he flew over the cottage, his sharp eyes saw something—a magic cloud of pink. Then out came another magic cloud—but this one was blue! Sput—pink! Sput—blue! Pink! Blue! Pink! Blue!

Down came the raven and alighted on the chimney's edge. He leaned forward and—Sput! A cloud of pink magic hit him in the face!

Away Maleficent's raven flew, bright pink, just as Briar Rose came singing down the path. He had seen magic in the woods and that was enough.

"Not pink!" cried Merryweather, as she stepped back to look at the dress, which had been made by magic. "Oh, no! Let's make it blue!" And with a flash of her wand, she changed the color of the dress.

"Pink!" cried Flora, changing it back.

"Blue!" cried Merryweather. And so it went. The fairies did not realize that puffs of pink and blue magic were spouting from the chimney with each flash of their wands.

It happened that a raven was flying over the forest, and this raven was Maleficent's pet bird. He had been sent out to find the Princess before the sixteen-year curse ran out. And this was the very last day. He shivered uneasily thinking of what Maleficent would do to him if he did not succeed in his task.

"Once upon a dream," Briar Rose was singing as she opened the cottage door. "Aunt Flora," she called, eager to share her happy news. "Fauna! Merryweather! Where is everybody?"

Then she saw the new dress draped on a chair. And she saw the magic layer cake on the table.

"Oh! How lovely!" Briar Rose said.

"Surprise!" cried the fairies, popping out from their hiding places. "Happy birthday!"

"Oh, you darlings," said Briar Rose. "This is the happiest day of my life. Everything is so wonderful. Just wait till you meet him."

"Him?" gasped the fairies. "You've met some stranger?"

"Oh, he's not a stranger," Briar Rose said. "We've met before."

"Where?" asked the fairies.

"Once upon a dream," sighed Briar Rose, closing her eyes.

"She's in love!" cried Fauna.

"Oh, no!" cried Merryweather.

"This is terrible," wailed Flora.

"But why?" asked Briar Rose. "After all, I am sixteen."

"But you're already betrothed," Flora explained sadly. "You have been since the day you were born, to Prince Phillip."

"That's impossible," said Briar Rose. "To marry a Prince, I'd have to be a—"

"Princess," broke in Merryweather. "And you are, dear. You are Princess Aurora. And tonight we are taking you home to your father, King Stefan."

"I can't go," said Briar Rose. "He's coming here tonight. I asked him to call."

"I'm sorry, child," said Fauna kindly. "But you must never see your young man again."

"Oh, no, no!" sobbed Briar Rose, bursting into tears. And she stumbled up the stairs to her room.

Behind her the three fairies stood staring unhappily at the cake and dress.

"And we thought she'd be so pleased," Merryweather sighed.

The golden light of the late afternoon warmed the ancient castle walls as the three fairies hurried an unhappy Briar Rose up side roads and byways to her rightful home.

Shadows were deepening around them as they slipped into the courtyard by a small door. Unseen and silent, they quickly crossed the courtyard and disappeared through a shadowy archway into the castle itself. Then down dim halls and up circular stairs they went. And at last Flora, who was leading them, opened the door to the Princess's own room.

"All right, dear," Flora whispered. "In here." And in they went, very quietly and all on tiptoe.

"Bolt the doors, Merryweather," Flora ordered. "Fauna, pull the drapes. Until the evening sun has set, we are not safe from Maleficent or the curse." Flora's bright gaze

darted to every side. Not a sign of danger did she see.

"Sit down, dear," said Flora, "and make yourself at home while we go to see your father to find out if—if there is anything more we can do."

What the loving fairies hoped was that they could find a way to make the Princess's dream of seeing her young man again come true. So off they fluttered, leaving Briar Rose —or Princess Aurora, as she was called in the castle—sobbing in the dim and lonely dusk.

The very day her dream of a wonderful stranger came to life, the day of her birthday, was turning out to be the unhappiest day of the Princess's life.

Meanwhile the castle of King Stefan was all a-bustle. There was not a person in the country who did not know that today was the day Princess Aurora was coming home.

The news had traveled far beyond the country's borders. King Hubert of the neighboring kingdom had already arrived at the castle. For, as everyone knew, at the birthday ball the wedding of the young Princess Aurora and her Prince would be announced.

In the royal study, King Stefan and King Hubert were busy with plans.

"And we've already built a cottage," Hubert said. "The lovebirds can move in tomorrow. Nothing elaborate, of course. Just forty bedrooms, ten dining halls, and—"

"But Hubert," said Stefan sadly, "I haven't even seen my daughter yet. And you're taking her away from me!"

They were interrupted by a herald's shout: "His Royal Highness, Prince Phillip!"

"My son!" cried Hubert. He raced to greet the Prince.

"Hurry, son," Hubert said. "Change into something suitable. You can't meet your future bride looking like that."

"But I have met her, father," said Phillip.

King Hubert was almost speechless with surprise. "You have?" he gasped. "But where?"

"Oh, once upon a dream," sang Phillip.

"Stop all this nonsense about dreams," snapped his father.

"But it wasn't only a dream, father," said Phillip more seriously. "I really did meet her."

"The Princess Aurora?" said his father. "Good heavens, we must tell Stefan."

"I didn't say it was Aurora," Phillip reminded him. "I said I met the girl I am going to marry. I don't know who she was—a peasant girl, I suppose."

"A peasant girl!" cried King Hubert. "You're going to marry—Oh, Phillip, you're joking, of course."

But Prince Phillip was not joking.

"You can't do this to me!" his father said. "You're a prince and you're going to marry a princess! I won't have it!"

"Now, father," said Phillip, "you're living in the past. This is the fourteenth century. And I am going to marry the girl I love, even if it means giving up the throne."

"Nonsense!" said King Hubert.

"Very well," said Phillip. And with a shrug of his shoulders, he swung himself up into Samson's saddle and turned away.

"Phillip!" said his father. "Come back, son!"

But Phillip was out of the castle gates and off on the road to the woods.

Behind him King Hubert sank down on the steps, holding his head in his hands. "How will I ever tell Stefan," he moaned.

But worse was still to come.

Unaware of all that was going on, Aurora still sobbed in her room. Then a thread of melody drifted into the room and made her feel warm and soothed.

The melody beckoned. As if in a spell, Aurora followed it. The fireplace opened and she mounted the stairs behind it.

Even the fairies heard the music. But by the time they raced back into the room, Aurora had already disappeared up the magic stairs. They were too late.

Meanwhile, the Princess, still under a spell, moved toward the shadows where Maleficent stood near a spinning wheel.

"Don't touch anything!" the fairies called.

But Maleficent's evil voice rang out:

"Touch the spindle!"

Aurora sleepily stretched out her hand.

Prick! The spindle scratched her skin. Aurora crumpled to the floor.

"You poor simple fools," Maleficent sneered at the fairies, "thinking that your puny powers could defeat me." And with an evil laugh, Maleficent vanished in a puff of black smoke.

"Poor King Stefan," sighed Fauna. "And the Queen. They'll be heartbroken when they find out."

"They're not going to find out," said Flora. "We'll put them all to sleep until the Princess awakens."

Off the fairies flew through the castle, scattering their magic stardust, until everyone in the castle was wrapped in a blanket of magic, peaceful sleep.

Just as the fairies left the castle, Prince Phillip was coming to the tiny cottage in the woods.

But it was not the girl he loved who waited behind the curtains. It was Maleficent.

Outside Phillip squared his shoulders, straightened his cloak, and knocked at the cottage door.

"Come in," called Maleficent sweetly.

Phillip swung the door open and stepped inside.

And before Phillip, blinking at the darkness, could tell what was happening, Maleficent cried out, "Away with him!"

And from the darkness on every side evil spirits came swooping. Soon Phillip and Samson were helplessly caught in their nets. Then away the evil spirits flew, bearing their captives to the dismal dungeons of Maleficent's castle of darkness.

Soon after, but too late, the three fairies pushed open the door. They knew immediately that something was wrong.

"Maleficent!" they cried out together, when they saw the prince's hat. And without a thought for their own safety, they flew off through the woods towards the castle of Maleficent.

Meanwhile, Maleficent taunted Phillip, her great black cape billowing about her.

"Think," Maleficent said, "that in the topmost tower of King Stefan's castle the Princess Aurora sleeps—and she is the selfsame peasant maid who won your heart just yesterday in the forest glade."

Phillip looked up in surprise. The Princess Aurora his own true love? And here he was a prisoner!

"She is indeed most wondrous fair," Maleficent's cruel voice went on. "And she will sleep through the ages, lacking this—the magic of her true love's kiss!"

Her true love's kiss! Phillip sprang to his feet. He must go to her! But his chains held him back.

Phillip held his head in his hands while Maleficent laughed.

"Come, my pet," Maleficent whispered to her pet raven, "let us leave our noble prince with his thoughts."

Soon the dungeon door clanked shut behind them. Phillip and Samson were left alone in the dark.

At last the good fairies reached the castle of evil. Down they flew into the deep dungeon.

"How did you get here?" Phillip asked.

"Shh!" said Flora. "No time to explain."

Sparks shot out from the three tiny wands and the Prince's chains fell off.

"Now," said Flora, "be on your way armed with this enchanted shield of virtue and this mighty sword of truth. For these are the weapons of good that will win over evil."

Phillip sprang to Samson's back and away he galloped.

Hearing him, Maleficent screamed with rage, "Up with the drawbridge!"

On raced Samson. Up swung the bridge. A deep chasm lay below. The horse gathered himself for a mighty leap and carried Phillip safely to the farther side.

As Prince Phillip vanished from her sight, Maleficent's face twisted with anger. She cried into the darkness:

"Poison thorn and witch's knell
Round Stefan's castle cast my spell!"

The good fairies, flying at the prince's side, were the first to see the terrible hedge of thorns.

"The sword of truth!" they called out. "Its power will cut through the hedge."

Slash! Slash! Phillip swung the sword this

But the good fairies swooped up the shield and slipped it over Phillip's arm, and they slid the sword of truth to within his reach.

"Swish!" came the dragon's fiery breath. But the shield of virtue turned back the flames. Slash! came the dragon's sharp teeth. But the Prince struck with his sword.

The dreadful dragon of evil lay slain. And the Prince led Samson up to the gate of the great castle.

With the help of the good fairies, Prince

way and that. Soon he cleared a hole in the hedge just big enough for Samson to leap through.

"The castle at last!" Phillip said.

But Maleficent had not given up. And before Phillip's eyes, a huge fire-breathing dragon reared its head.

It flung Phillip from Samson's saddle. Down fell the sword of truth and the shield of virtue.

Phillip found his way through the castle, right to the room where Aurora lay asleep.

For a moment the prince stood staring. She was even more lovely than he had remembered. Then, kneeling, he bent over her. Princess Aurora awakened at the touch of love's first kiss.

All through the sleeping castle went a sigh. The torch bearers awoke and stretched. In the courtyard the fountain awoke with a flutter of tinkling drops. In the kitchens the cooks all rubbed their eyes and dipped their spoons into bubbling pots again.

And in the throne room, King Hubert, King Stefan, and King Stefan's Queen were dozing side by side.

Stefan awoke first. "Forgive me, Hubert!" he said to his guest, "You were saying—?"

"Er—uh," yawned Hubert rousing slowly. "I was?" Then he remembered his scene with Prince Phillip. It seemed so long ago! But he still had to face his bitter task. He still had to tell Stefan that his son Phillip refused to marry Stefan's daughter Aurora.

"Oh, yes," Hubert began vaguely. "After all, Stefan, this is the fourteenth century."

"You said that," said Stefan, "a moment ago."

"Well, what I mean is," said Hubert. "Oh, dash it, to come right to the point, my son Phillip says he's going to marry—"

A blare of trumpets interrupted him, and

the voice of the royal herald rang through the hall.

"Their royal highness, Princess Aurora and Prince Phillip!"

And, to the music of the royal orchestra, Princess Aurora made her first appearance on the arm of her true love, the handsome young Prince.

King Stefan and his Queen watched wide-eyed as their lovely daughter came toward them down the grand staircase.

"It's Aurora!" said Stefan. His hand was trembling. "She's here!"

Hubert turned to look. He rubbed his eyes. Then he smiled proudly. The young man was Phillip.

Meanwhile, from a balcony high above, the three good fairies looked down happily.

Their beloved Briar Rose, now Princess Aurora, was reunited with her parents after sixteen long years.

There were tears of joy in King Hubert's eyes as he watched the happy scene. But when he turned to his tall young son, he tried to make his voice sound stern.

"What does this mean?" Hubert asked. "I simply don't understand."

"It's the happy ending, father," Prince Phillip explained. "The happy ending to a story that started once upon a dream."

Then Prince Phillip caught the Princess by the hand. To the swelling music of the royal orchestra, they waltzed into the land of their dreams. There they lived happily ever after, you may be sure.

High above them the fairies watched. Fauna dabbed at her eyes.

"What is the matter, dear?" her sister Flora asked.

"Oh," sniffed Fauna. "I love happy endings." And her tears fell.

"Yes," sighed Flora, wiping her own eyes, "so do I."

But, just then, Flora's eye fell on the Princess's gown.

"Oh dear! Blue!" she said. And at the flash of her magic wand, the gown turned to pink.

Merryweather had been watching the dancing. But as the gown turned pink, she gasped. Up came her wand.

"Blue!" she whispered.

And that was how it happened that, as she danced, the Princess's gown kept flashing from blue to pink to blue, right up to

THE END

PINOCCHIO

ONE NIGHT, long, long ago, the Evening Star shone down across the dark sky. Its beams formed a shimmering pathway to a tiny village, and painted its humble roofs with stardust.

But the silent little town was deep in sleep. The only witness to the beauty of the night was a weary wayfarer who chanced to be passing through.

His clothes were gray with dust. His well-worn shoes pinched his feet; his back ached from the weight of the carpetbag slung over his shabby shoulder. To be sure, it was only a small carpetbag; but this wayfarer had a very small shoulder. As a matter of fact, he was an exceedingly small wayfarer. His name was Cricket, Jiminy Cricket.

He marveled at the radiant star; it seemed almost close enough to touch, and pretty as a picture. But at this moment Jiminy Cricket was not interested in pretty pictures. He was looking for a place to rest.

Suddenly he noticed a light in a window, and smoke curling from a chimney.

"Where there's smoke, there's a fire," he reasoned. "Where there's a fire, there's a hearth. And where there's a hearth, there *should* be a cricket!"

And with that, he hopped up to the window sill and peered in. The room had a friendly look. So Jiminy crawled under the door, scurried over to the hearth, backed up against the glowing fireplace, and warmed his little britches.

It was no ordinary village home into which the small wayfarer had stumbled. It was a workshop: the workshop of Geppetto the woodcarver. Old Geppetto was working late that night. He was making a puppet.

Geppetto lived alone except for his black kitten, Figaro, and a pet goldfish he called Cleo. But he had many friends; everyone knew and loved the kindly, white-haired old man. He had spent his whole life creating happiness for others.

It was the children who loved Geppetto best. He doctored their dolls, put clean sawdust into limp rag bodies and painted fresh smiles on faded china faces. He fashioned new arms and legs for battered tin soldiers—and there was magic in his hands when he carved a toy.

Now, the weary old fellow put his tools away and surveyed his newest handiwork. The puppet he had made had the figure of a small boy. He was the right size for a small boy. He had the cute, round face of a small boy—except for one feature. The nose! Geppetto had given him a very long and pointed nose, such a nose as no real boy ever possessed. A funny nose.

The old woodcarver stroked his chin and chuckled. "Woodenhead," he said, "you are finished, and you deserve a name. What shall I call you? I know—*Pinocchio!* Do you like it?" He worked the puppet's strings so that it nodded "Yes."

"That settles it!" cried Geppetto happily. "Pinocchio you are! And now," he yawned, "time for bed. Good night, Figaro! Good night, Cleo! Good night, Pinocchio!"

Jiminy Cricket was glad to hear these words, for he felt very sleepy. Geppetto put on a long white nightshirt and climbed creakily into bed, but he still sat admiring the puppet with its wooden smile.

"Look at him, Figaro!" he exclaimed. "He seems almost real. Wouldn't it be nice if he were alive?"

But the only answer from the kitten was a snore.

Long after Geppetto had gone to sleep, Jiminy Cricket lay awake thinking. It made him sad to realize the old man's wish could never come true.

Suddenly he heard something. Music—mysterious music! He sat up and looked around the room. Then he saw a strange light—a brilliant glow, which grew more dazzling every minute. It was a star—the Evening Star, floating down the sky and entering Geppetto's window!

Then in the center of its blinding glow appeared a beautiful lady dressed in robes of flowing blue.

"As I live and breathe!" Jiminy whispered in astonishment. "A fairy!"

The Blue Fairy bent over the old woodcarver and spoke to him ever so softly, so as not to disturb his slumber.

"Good Geppetto," she said, "you have given so much happiness to others, you deserve to have your wish come true!"

Then she turned to the wooden puppet. Holding out her glittering wand, she spoke these words:

> *Little puppet made of pine,*
> *Wake! The gift of life is thine!"*

And when the wand touched him, Pinocchio came to life! First he blinked his eyes, then he raised his wooden arm and wiggled his jointed fingers.

"I can move!" he cried. "I can *talk*!"

"Yes, Pinocchio," the Blue Fairy smiled. "Geppetto needs a little son. So tonight I give you life."

"Then I'm a real boy!" cried Pinocchio.

"No," said the Fairy sadly. "There is no magic that can make us real. I have given you life—the rest is up to you."

"Tell me what I must do," begged Pinocchio. "I want to be a real boy!"

"Prove yourself brave, truthful, and un-selfish," said the Blue Fairy. "Be a good son to Geppetto—make him proud of you! Then, some day, you will wake up and find yourself a real boy!"

"Whew! That won't be easy," thought Jiminy Cricket.

But the Blue Fairy also realized what a hard task she was giving Pinocchio. "The world is full of temptations," she continued. "You must learn to choose between right and wrong—"

"Right? Wrong?" questioned Pinocchio. "How will I know?"

Jiminy wrung his hands in desperation. But the wise Fairy was not yet finished. "Your conscience will tell you the difference between right and wrong," she explained.

"What is conscience?" Pinocchio asked.

That was too much for Jiminy Cricket. He hopped down where he could be seen.

"A conscience," he shouted, "is that still small voice people won't listen to! That's the trouble with the world today!"

"Are *you* my conscience?" asked Pinocchio eagerly.

Jiminy was embarrassed, but the Blue Fairy came to his rescue. "Would you like to be Pinocchio's conscience?" she smiled. "You seem a man of the world. What is your name?"

Jiminy was flattered. "Jiminy Cricket," he answered.

"Kneel, Mister Cricket," commanded the Blue Fairy and Jiminy knelt.

"I dub you Pinocchio's conscience," she proclaimed, "Lord High Keeper of the Knowledge of Right and Wrong! Arise—*Sir* Jiminy Cricket!"

And when the dusty little cricket rose his shabby old clothes were gone and he was clad in elegant raiment from head to foot.

"Don't I get a badge or something?" he asked.

"We'll see," the Blue Fairy smiled.

"Make it a gold one?" urged Jiminy.

"Perhaps, if you do your job well," she said. "I leave Pinocchio in your hands. Give him the benefit of your advice and experience. Help him to be a real boy!"

It was a serious moment for the little cricket. He promised to help Pinocchio as much as he could, and to stick by him through thick and thin. The Blue Fairy thanked him.

"And now, Pinocchio," she said, "be a good boy—and always let your conscience be your guide! Don't be discouraged because you are different from the other boys! Remember—*any child who is not good, might just as well be made of wood!*" The Blue Fairy backed slowly away. There was one last soft chord of music and she was gone.

Pinocchio and Jiminy stared silently at the spot where the Fairy had stood, half hoping she might return. The little cricket finally broke the spell.

"Say, she's all right, son!" he exclaimed. "Remember what she told you—always let your conscience be your guide!"

"Yes sir, I will!" answered Pinocchio.

"And when you need me, whistle," said Jiminy, "like this!"

"Like this?" Pinocchio tried, but no sound came.

So Jiminy sang him a little lecture-lesson, which went something like this:

"When you get in trouble
And you don't know
  right from wrong,
Give a little whistle,
Give a little whistle.
When you meet temptation
And the urge is very strong,
Give a little whistle,
Give a little whistle.

Then he began dancing down the strings of a violin on the bench, balancing himself with his small umbrella.

"Take the straight and narrow path
And if you start to slide,
Give a little whistle,
Give a little whistle—"

Just then the violin string broke. Jiminy fell over backward, but picked himself up and finished, "and always let your conscience be your guide!"

Pinocchio watched entranced as the little cricket went on dancing. Finally he too jumped up and tried to make his wooden feet go through the same steps. But he danced too close to the edge of the workbench, lost his balance and fell clatteringly to the floor.

The noise woke Geppetto. "Who's there?" he called.

Pinocchio, on the floor, answered, "It's *me!*"

Geppetto's teeth chattered with fright. "Figaro, there's somebody in here!" he whispered. "A burglar, maybe! Come, we'll catch him!"

Then to his surprise, he noticed his puppet, which he had left on the workbench, lying on the floor.

"Why, Pinocchio!" he exclaimed. "How did you get down there?" He picked the puppet up and set him back on the bench. Imagine his surprise when Pinocchio answered!

"I fell down!" he said.

Geppetto stared. "What! You're talking?" he cried. "No! You're only a marionette. You can't talk!"

"Yes, I can," insisted the puppet. "I can move, too!"

The old man backed away. "No, no," he argued. "I must be dreaming! I will pour water on myself! I will stick me with pins!"

Geppetto made sure he was awake. "Now we will see who is dreaming," he challenged. "Go on—say something!"

Pinocchio laughed merrily. "Do it again!" he begged. "You're very funny! I like you!"

"You *do* talk," said the old man, in a hushed voice. "Pinocchio! It's a miracle! Figaro! Cleo! Look—he's alive!"

Geppetto didn't know whether to laugh or cry, he was so happy. "This calls for a celebration!" he announced. He turned on a music box and began to dance. He went to his toy shelves and filled his arms with playthings. It was just like Christmas for Pinocchio. He couldn't decide which toy to play with first.

But the music box ran down and the celebration ended.

"Now it is time for bed," said the old woodcarver. "Come, Pinocchio. You shall sleep here in this dresser drawer." He tucked Pinocchio in and said, "Sleep fast, Pinocchio!"

That night Jiminy Cricket did an unusual thing—for him. He prayed. He prayed that Pinocchio might never disappoint that kind, happy old man or the lovely Blue Fairy, and that he himself might be a good conscience, so Pinocchio would soon earn the right to be a real boy.

All was still in the little shop. High in the sky the Evening Star twinkled softly, as though smiling approval of a good night's work.

Morning dawned bright and clear. As the school bells rang out over the village, their clamor sent pigeons flying from the old belfry like colored fans spread against the white clouds.

The school bells carried a special message of joy to old Geppetto. Today his own son was to join the other little ones on their way to school!

Pinocchio too was impatient. His face, shiny from scrubbing, beamed with excitement. Even Figaro and Cleo realized it was a gala day.

At last Pinocchio was pronounced ready. Geppetto opened the door. For the first time the puppet looked out at the wide, wide world. How beautiful it was!

"What are those?" he asked, pointing down the street.

"Those are the children, bless them!" Geppetto answered. "They are the boys and girls—your schoolmates, Pinocchio!"

"Real boys?" Pinocchio asked eagerly.

"Yes, my son. And if you study hard, you'll soon be as smart as they are. Wait a minute—your books!"

Little Figaro appeared at the door, tugging the strap which held Pinocchio's schoolbooks.

"Ah, thank you, Figaro. You too want to help! Pinocchio, here are your books. Remember, be a good boy. Choose your friends carefully; shun evil companions. Mind the teacher—"

"Good-bye!" shouted Pinocchio, pulling carelessly away. But he thought better of it, ran back and threw his arms around Geppetto. "Good-bye, Father," he said shyly; then off he marched, his books under his arm, chock-full of good resolutions.

Jiminy Cricket heard the school bell and jumped up in a great hurry. Suppose Pinocchio had gone off to school without him! If ever a small boy needs a conscience, it is on his first day at school. A fine time to oversleep, Jiminy thought. Then he stuffed

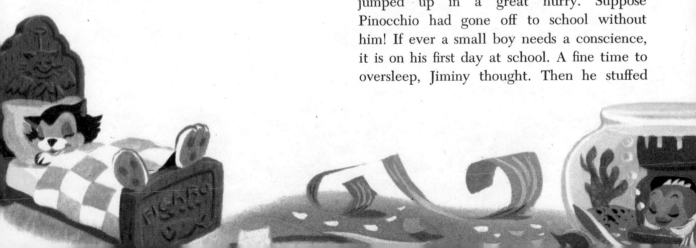

his shirt hastily inside his trousers, grabbed his hat and rushed out.

"Hey, Pinoke!" he called. "Wait for me!"

"An extra mouth to feed, Figaro," Geppetto chuckled cheerfully to the kitten. "Yet what a joy it is to have someone to work for!"

But alas, many a dreary day and night were to pass before the old woodcarver saw his boy again! For in spite of Geppetto's warning, Pinocchio fell into bad company. He met two scheming adventurers—a Fox and a Cat, the worst pair of scoundrels in the whole countryside.

Run down at the heel and patched at the seat, these villains managed somehow to look like elegant gentlemen out for a stroll. But as usual, they were up to no good.

Suddenly, "Look!" cried the sharp-eyed Fox, who went by the name of J. Worthington Foulfellow, alias Honest John. "Do you see what I see?" He pointed with his cane. The stupid Cat, who was called Gideon, stared at Pinocchio.

"A puppet that walks!" marveled Foulfellow. "A live puppet—a marionette without strings! A breathing woodenhead!"

And before Pinocchio knew what had happened, he was lying flat on his face. Something had tripped him up, and that something was a cane, thrust between his feet by the sly old fox.

"My dear young man! I'm so sorry," Foulfellow apologized, helping Pinocchio to his feet. "A most regrettable accident—Mr.—er—"

"Pinocchio," answered the little puppet cheerfully.

"Ha ha, Pinocchio," began Foulfellow, "you were going a little too fast! A little too fast, and in the *wrong* direction. Now I have a plan for you. Come . . ."

"But I'm on my way to school," said Pinocchio.

"To school? Nonsense!" said Foulfellow. "I have a much better plan."

"You're too bright a boy to waste your time in school," said Foulfellow. "Isn't he, Gideon?" Gideon nodded.

"You deserve a trip to Pleasure Island, my boy," said sly old Foulfellow.

"Pleasure Island?" repeated Pinocchio.

"Pleasure Island!" cried Foulfellow. "Where every day is a holiday, with fireworks, brass bands, parades—a paradise for boys! Why, I can see you now—lolling under a doughnut tree, a lollipop in each hand, gazing off at the pink Ice Cream Mountains —think of it, Pinocchio!"

It was a tempting picture the sly fox painted. "Well, I *was* going to school," said Pinocchio. He hesitated. "But perhaps I could go to Pleasure Island first—for a little while . . ."

"Oh, what a woodenhead he is!" thought Jiminy Cricket, panting along behind. He was too late to stop the three of them strolling off together.

So he loyally followed.

Soon they came to a great coach, piled to the brim with boys—eager, noisy, impudent boys! Laughing and shouting, Pinocchio climbed aboard.

"Good-bye!" Pinocchio called to the Fox. "I'll never be able to thank you for this!"

"Think nothing of it, my boy," said the Fox. "Seeing you happy is our only reward. Our only reward—reward—*reward!*" he kept repeating, until the wicked-looking Coachman slipped him a large sack of gold. The Fox had sold Pinocchio for gold!

Jiminy Cricket saw the Coachman crack his long blacksnake whip, and the coach start to move. The coach was drawn by eight sorrowful-looking little donkeys, who seemed to feel very badly. "Tsk! Tsk! Tsk!" they said, every time the Coachman's whip descended. But nobody could hear them because of the boys' shouting.

"Three cheers for anything," they yelled, throwing their caps into the air as the coach rolled away. "Hurray for Pleasure Island!"

Jiminy made a last desperate effort. He hopped onto the rear axle of the coach and rode along. Certain that Pinocchio was headed for disaster, the loyal little cricket went with him just the same.

The journey was an unhappy one for Jiminy. At the waterfront, the passengers boarded a ferryboat for Pleasure Island, and the little cricket suffered from seasickness during the entire voyage.

But physical discomfort was not what bothered him most. He was worried about Pinocchio, who promptly made friends with the worst boy in the crowd—a no-good named "Lampwick." Lampwick talked out of the corner of his mouth, and was very untidy. Yet Pinocchio cherished his friendship.

Jiminy tried to warn Pinocchio, but the heedless puppet refused to listen. Finally the ferry docked and the boys swarmed down the gangplank onto Pleasure Island.

Bands played loudly; wonderful circuses performed along the streets, which were paved with cookies and lined with doughnut trees. Lollipops and cupcakes grew on bushes, and fountains spouted lemonade and soda pop. The Mayor of Pleasure Island made a speech of welcome and urged the boys to enjoy themselves.

Yes, Pleasure Island seemed to be all the Fox had claimed for it, and more. Only Jiminy Cricket was skeptical. He felt that there was more to all this than appeared on the surface. But weeks went by, and seldom did Jiminy get close enough to Pinocchio to warn him. He was always in the midst of the fun, and his friend Lampwick was the ringleader of the horde of mischievous boys.

They smashed windows and burned schoolbooks; in fact they did whatever they felt like doing, no matter how destructive. They ate until they nearly burst. And always the Coachman and Mayor encouraged them to "Have a good time—while you can!"

And all the while the poor little donkeys—who performed all the hard labor on the island—looked very sad and said "Tsk! Tsk!!"

One day Pinocchio and Lampwick were lazily floating in a canoe along the Lemonade River, which flowed between the Ice Cream Mountains. Chocolate cattails grew thickly along the banks, lollipop trees drooped overhead, and the canoe was piled high with sweets.

"This is too good to be true, Lampwick," Pinocchio sighed blissfully. "I could stay here forever."

"Aw, this is kid stuff," retorted Lampwick. "Let's go where we can have some real fun!"

"Where?" asked Pinocchio curiously.

"I'll show you," said Lampwick. So they pulled the canoe up on the bank, and Lampwick then led the way to Tobacco Lane.

Here the fences were made of cigars, cigarettes and matches grew on bushes, and there were rows of cornstalks with corncob pipes on them. Lampwick lit a cigar and began smoking.

Pinocchio hesitated. Finally he picked a corncob pipe and began to puff timidly.

"Aw, you smoke like my granmudder," jeered Lampwick. "Take a big drag, Pinoke —like dis!"

Under Lampwick's instruction, Pinocchio soon found himself smoking like a chimney. Just then, along came Jiminy. How sad the little cricket felt when he saw this you will never know. While he had known for a long time that Pinocchio had fallen into evil ways, Jiminy did not realize he had sunk to such depths.

Well, he had tried everything—except force. Would that make the lad come to his senses? He decided to try. He shook his little fist angrily. "So it's come to this, has it?" he shouted. "SMOKING!"

Pinocchio gave him a careless glance. "Yeah," he answered out of the corner of his mouth, in imitation of Lampwick. "So what?"

"Just this!" Jiminy exploded. "You're making a disgusting spectacle of yourself. You're going home this minute!"

Lampwick, who had never seen Jiminy before, was curious. "Who's de insect, Pinoke?"

"Jiminy? Why, he's my conscience," explained Pinocchio.

Lampwick began to laugh. "You mean you take advice from a *beetle?*" he remarked insultingly. "Say, I can't waste time wid a sap like you. So long!" And he strolled away.

"Lampwick! Don't go!" cried Pinocchio. "Now see what you've done, Jiminy! Lampwick was my best friend!"

That was too much for the little cricket. "So *he's* your best friend," he said angrily. "Well, Pinocchio, that's the last straw. I'm through! I'm taking the next boat!"

Pinocchio hesitated but temptation was too strong. He couldn't give Lampwick up. He started off after him, full of apologies.

"Hey wait, Lampwick!" he called. "I'm coming with *you!*"

That was the end as far as Jiminy was concerned. "So he prefers to remain with that hoodlum, and allow him to insult *me*, his conscience?" he muttered. "Well, from now on he can paddle his own canoe. I'm going home!"

And he started toward the entrance gate, so upset that he did not notice how dark and forlorn Pleasure Island looked. There wasn't a boy in sight on the wide streets.

Jiminy's only thought was to get away quickly. He was just about to pound angrily on the gate when he heard voices on the other side. He tried to listen, and became conscious of a reddish glow which cast great, frightening shadows against the high stone walls. The shadows looked like prison guards, and they carried guns!

Jiminy jumped up and peered fearfully through the keyhole. In the cove, lit by flaming torches, he saw something that made his blood turn cold.

The ferryboat stood waiting, stripped of its decorations. The dock swarmed with howling, braying donkeys—fat ones and thin ones, many of whom still wore boys' hats and shoes. Huge, ape-like guards herded them into crates, assisted by the Coachman, who cracked his whip brutally over the poor donkeys' heads.

The little cricket shuddered. At last he understood the meaning of Pleasure Island. This, then, was what became of lazy, good-for-nothing boys! They made donkeys of themselves! This was Pinocchio's fate, unless—

Forgetting his anger, Jiminy leaped to the ground and started back toward Tobacco Lane. He must warn Pinocchio at once.

"Pinocchio!" he yelled. "Pinocchio!" But his cries only echoed through the empty streets.

Not far away, Pinocchio was still looking for Lampwick. He wandered unhappily past pie trees and popcorn shrubs. The island suddenly seemed strange, deserted.

Then he heard a frightened voice say, "Here I am!"

"Lampwick!" Pinocchio answered joyfully. "Where are you?"

Just then a little donkey emerged from some bushes. "Ssh!" he whispered. "Stop yelling! They'll hear us!"

Pinocchio stared. The donkey spoke in Lampwick's voice!

"This is no time for jokes," Pinocchio said crossly. "What are you doing in that donkey suit?"

"This ain't no donkey suit, Pinoke," the frightened voice replied. "*I am* a donkey!"

Pinocchio laughed. "You a donkey?" For he still thought it was a joke. "Ha ha ha! *He-Haw! He-Haw! He-Haw!*"

Pinocchio turned pale, but he couldn't stop. He was braying like a donkey!

The little donkey came closer to him. "That's the first sign of donkey fever," he whispered. "That's how I started."

"Then—then you *are* Lampwick! What happened?"

"Donkey fever," replied Lampwick, "and you've got it too!"

Pinocchio's head began to buzz like a hive of bees. He reached up and felt something horrible. Two long, hairy ears were growing out of his head!

"You've got it all right!" whispered Lampwick. "Look behind you!"

Pinocchio looked and discovered that he had a long tail. He began to tremble, and was no longer able to stand up straight. Then he found himself on all fours.

"Help! Help!" he shrieked. "Jiminy! Jiminy Cricket!"

Jiminy ran toward them, but he saw that he was too late.

"Oh! Oh! Oh me, oh my!" he groaned. "Look at you! Come on! Let's get away from here before you're a complete donkey!"

This time nobody argued with the little cricket. As he fled toward the high stone wall, Pinocchio and the donkey that had once been Lampwick followed as fast as their legs would carry them. But as they rounded a corner, they came face to face with the Coachman and his armed guards. They turned and dashed toward the opposite wall.

"There they go! That's the two that's missing!" yelled the Coachman. "After them! Sound the alarm!"

Instantly the air was filled with the sound of sirens and the baying of bloodhounds. Searchlights began to play over the island, and bullets whizzed past the ears of the escaping prisoners. They expected any minute to be shot.

Pinocchio and Jiminy reached the wall and managed to climb to the top before the ape-like guards got within shooting distance. But Lampwick, with his donkey hoofs, could not climb.

"Go on, Pinoke!" he cried. "It's all over with me!"

A lump came in Pinocchio's throat. After all, Lampwick was his friend. But there was nothing he could do. He turned his back and said a silent prayer. Then he and Jiminy dove into the sea.

Bullets splashed all around them in the

water, but by some miracle neither of them was hit. Finally a thick fog hid them from the glaring searchlights, and the sound of the guns died away. They had escaped!

It was a long, hard swim back to the mainland. When they reached shore,

Pinocchio longed to see once more the cozy little cottage and his dear, kind father. Pleasure Island, and all it stood for, now seemed like a bad dream. But they were by no means at the end of their journey, for home was still many weary miles away.

It was winter when at last one evening they limped into the village. They hurried through the drifting snow to Geppetto's shop. Eagerly, Pinocchio pounded on the door.

"Father! Father!" he cried. "It's me! It's Pinocchio!"

But the only reply was the howling of the wintry wind.

"He must be asleep," said Pinocchio, and he knocked again. But again there was no answer.

Worried, Pinocchio hastened to the window and peered in. The house was empty! Everything was shrouded and dusty.

"He's gone, Jiminy," said Pinocchio sorrowfully. "My father's gone away!"

"Looks like he's gone for good, too," said Jiminy. "What'll we do?"

"I don't know." Pinocchio sat down on the doorstep shivering. A tear came from his eye, ran down his long nose and froze into a tiny, sparkling icicle. But Pinocchio didn't even bother to wipe it off. He felt terrible.

Just then a gust of wind blew around the corner, carrying a piece of paper. Jiminy hopped over to see what it was.

"Hey, Pinoke, it's a letter!" he exclaimed.

"Oh! Maybe it's from my father!" cried Pinocchio, and he quickly took the note from Jiminy and tried to read it. But alas, the marks on the paper meant nothing.

"You see, if you had gone to school you could read your father's letter," Jiminy reminded him. "Here—give it to me!"

The little cricket began to read the note aloud, and this is what it said:

"Dear Pinocchio:

"I heard you had gone to Pleasure Island, so I got a small boat and started off to search for you. Everyone said it was a dangerous voyage, but Figaro, Cleo, and I thought we could reach you and save you from a terrible fate.

"We weathered the storms, and finally reached the Terrible Straits. But just as we came in sight of our goal, out of the sea rose Monstro, the Terror of the Deep—the giant whale who swallows ships whole. He opened his jaws. In we went—boat and all . . ."

Here Pinocchio's sobs interrupted Jiminy's reading of the letter as he realized Geppetto's plight.

"Oh, my poor, poor father!" the puppet moaned. "He's dead! And it's all my fault!" He began to weep bitterly.

"But he isn't dead!" said Jiminy, and read on.

"So now, dear son, we are living at the bottom of the ocean in the belly of the whale. But there is very little to eat here, and we cannot exist much longer. So I fear you will never again see

Your loving father, GEPPETTO."

"Hurrah! Hurrah!" shouted Pinocchio.

"Hurrah for what?" asked Jiminy somewhat crossly. It did not seem to him to be quite the time for cheers.

"Don't you see, Jiminy?" cried Pinocchio. "My father is still alive! There may be time to save him!"

"Save him?" said Jiminy stupidly. Then suddenly a light dawned. "You don't mean *you*—"

"Yes!" announced Pinocchio. "I'm going after him. It's my fault he's down there in the whale; I'm going to the bottom of the ocean to rescue him!"

"But Pinocchio, you might be killed!" warned the cricket.

"I don't mind," declared Pinocchio. "What does life mean to me without my father? I've got to save him!"

Jiminy stared with open mouth. He hardly recognized this new Pinocchio—a brave, unselfish Pinocchio who stood there in place of the weak, foolish puppet he had always known.

"But think how far it is to the seashore—" he began.

Pinocchio looked thoughtful, but not for long. "I don't care. No place is too far for me to go after my father."

Just then, with a flutter of wings, a beautiful white dove settled gracefully down in the snow beside them.

"I will take you to the seashore," she said.

"You?" Pinocchio stared. But he did not see the tiny gold crown on the dove's head. It was she who had dropped the letter from the sky. She was his own dear Blue Fairy, disguised as a dove.

"Yes, I will help you," she assured him.

"How could a little dove carry me to the seashore?"

"Like this!"

And the dove began to grow and grow, until she was larger than an eagle. "Jump on my back," she commanded. Pinocchio obeyed.

"Good-bye, Jiminy Cricket," he said. "I may never see you again." He waved his hand to his little friend. "Thank you for all you've done!"

"Good-bye, nothing!" retorted Jiminy, and he too jumped on the back of the great white dove. "You're not leaving me! We'll see this through together!"

The dove raised her wide wings and rose from the ground. Higher and higher they flew, till the village disappeared and all they could see beneath them was whirling snow.

All night they flew through the storm. When morning came, the sun shone brightly. The dove's wings slowed down and she glided to earth at the edge of a cliff. Far below, the sea lay churning and lashing like a restless giant.

"I can take you no farther," said the dove. "Are you quite sure you want to go on this dangerous mission?"

"Yes," said Pinocchio. "Thank you for the ride. Good-bye!"

"Good-bye, Pinocchio," the dove replied. "Good luck!"

And she grew small again and flew away. Neither Pinocchio nor Jiminy realized that she was the Blue Fairy, but they were very grateful.

As soon as the dove was out of sight, Pinocchio tied a big stone to his donkey tail, to anchor him to the floor of the ocean. Then he smiled bravely at Jiminy and together they leaped off the cliff.

The weight of the stone caused Pinocchio to sink at once. By clinging desperately, little Jiminy managed to stay close by. They landed, picked themselves up and peered about. They were at the very bottom of the sea.

At first it seemed dark; they were many fathoms deep. Gradually Pinocchio's eyes became accustomed to the greenish light which filtered down into the submarine forest.

Giant clumps of seaweed waved overhead, like the branches of trees. Among them darted lovely bright objects, like birds or living flowers. They soon saw that these brilliant creatures were fish of all descriptions.

However, Pinocchio was in no frame of mind to make a study of the citizens of the sea. He walked along, peering into every cave and grotto in search of the great whale.

But the stone attached to his tail made him move slowly, and he grew impatient.

"I wish we knew just where to look," he thought. "Jiminy, where do you suppose Monstro might be?"

"Don't know, I'm sure," replied Jiminy. "I'll inquire here."

He knocked politely on an oyster. Its shell opened.

"Pardon me, Pearl," Jiminy began, "but could you tell me where we might find Monstro the Whale?"

To his surprise, the shell closed with a sharp click and the oyster scuttled off into a kelp bush as though frightened.

"Hm! That's funny!" remarked Jiminy.

Just then a school of tropical fish approached, brightly beautiful and extremely curious.

"I wonder," Pinocchio began, "if you could tell me where to find Monstro—"

But the lovely little creatures darted away before he had finished speaking. It was as though Pinocchio had threatened to harm them in some way.

A bit farther along, they encountered a herd of tiny sea horses, grazing on the sandy bottom. Pinocchio tried once more.

"Could you tell me," he asked, "where I might find Monstro the Whale?"

But the sea horses fled, their little ears raised in alarm.

"You know what I think?" exclaimed Jiminy. "I think everybody down here is afraid of Monstro! Why, they run away at the very mention of his name! He must be awful. Do you think we should go on?"

"Certainly!" declared Pinocchio. "I'm not afraid!"

So they went on. It was a strange journey. Sometimes the water grew very dark, and tiny phosphorescent fish glowed like fireflies in the depths. They learned to be careful not to step on the huge flowers which lay on the ocean's floor. For they were not flowers but sea anemones, which could reach up and capture whatever came within their grasp.

Striped fish glared at them from seaweed thickets like tigers in a jungle, and fish with horns and quills glowered at them. They saw wonders of the deep which no human eye has ever beheld—but nowhere could they find so much as one clue to the whereabouts of Monstro, the Terror of the Deep.

"The time is getting short!" said Pinocchio at last. "We must find him! My father will starve to death!"

"Father," he cried desperately. But there was no sound except the constant shifting and sighing of the watery depths.

"Let's go home, Pinocchio," Jiminy pleaded. "We'll never find Monstro in this big place. For all we know, we may be looking in the wrong ocean."

"No, Jiminy," said Pinocchio, "I'll never give up! Never!"

Not far away lay the Terror of the Deep, floating close to the surface, fast asleep. At times his broad back rose out of the water, to be mistaken for a desert island.

It was lucky for any ship close by that Monstro slept, for with but one flip of his tail he had been known to crush the sturdiest craft. As he snored the roars sounded like a tempest. It seemed impossible that anything could live within those crushing jaws.

Yet at the far end of the long, dark cavern formed by the whale's mouth lived a strange household: a kindly old man, whose skin was as pale as white paper, a small black kitten, whose ribs nearly pierced his fur, and a tiny, frightened goldfish, who swam weakly around in her bowl.

The old woodcarver had made his home on a shipwreck and furnished it with broken packing-cases from ships the whale had swallowed. He had salvaged a lantern, pots and pans and a few other necessities of life. But his stock of food was now very low; the lantern sputtering above his table was almost out of oil. The end was near.

Every day he fished in the mouth of the whale; but when Monstro slept, nothing entered that dark cavern. Now there was only a shallow pool of water, and it was useless to fish.

"Not a bite for days, Figaro," Geppetto said. "If Monstro doesn't wake up soon, it will be too bad for us. I never thought it would end like this!" He sighed mournfully. "Here we are, starving in the belly of a whale. And Pinocchio—poor, dear, little Pinocchio!" Geppetto was obliged to raise his thin voice to a shout, to be heard above the whale's snoring.

The old woodcarver looked tired and worn. He had never been so hungry in his whole life. Figaro was hungry too. He stared greedily at little Cleo, swimming slowly about her bowl.

As Geppetto went wearily back to his fishing, the kitten began to sneak toward Cleo's bowl. But the old man saw him.

"Scat!" shouted Geppetto. "You beast! You dog! Shame on you, Figaro, chasing Cleo, after the way I've brought you up!"

The hungry kitten scuttled away to a corner to try to forget the pangs whch gnawed him. Just then Geppetto felt a nibble at his line. He pulled it up in great excitement.

"It's a package, Figaro!" he cried. "Maybe it's food. Sausage, or cheese—"

But when the water-soaked package was unwrapped, it contained only a cook book! What a grim trick Fate had played!

"Oh, oh," groaned Geppetto. "I am so hungry! If we only had something to cook! Anything—"

He turned the pages, his mouth watering at the pictured recipes. "101 Ways to Cook

Fish," he read. Suddenly his eyes were drawn, as if by a magnet, to Cleo. He could almost see the melted butter sizzling! As in a nightmare, he walked toward the goldfish.

But as he started to scoop his little pet out and put her in the frying pan, the old man realized he could never do this thing.

"Dear Cleo," he begged, "forgive me! If we must die, let us die as we have lived—friends through thick and thin!"

It was a solemn moment. All felt that the end was near.

Then the whale moved!

"He's waking up!" cried Geppetto. "He's opening his mouth!"

Monstro gave an upward lunge, and through his jaws rushed a wall of black water. With it came fish—a whole school of fish! Hundreds of them.

"Food!" yelled Geppetto, seizing his pole. "Tuna fish! Oh, Figaro, Cleo—we are saved!"

And he began to pull fish after fish out of the water.

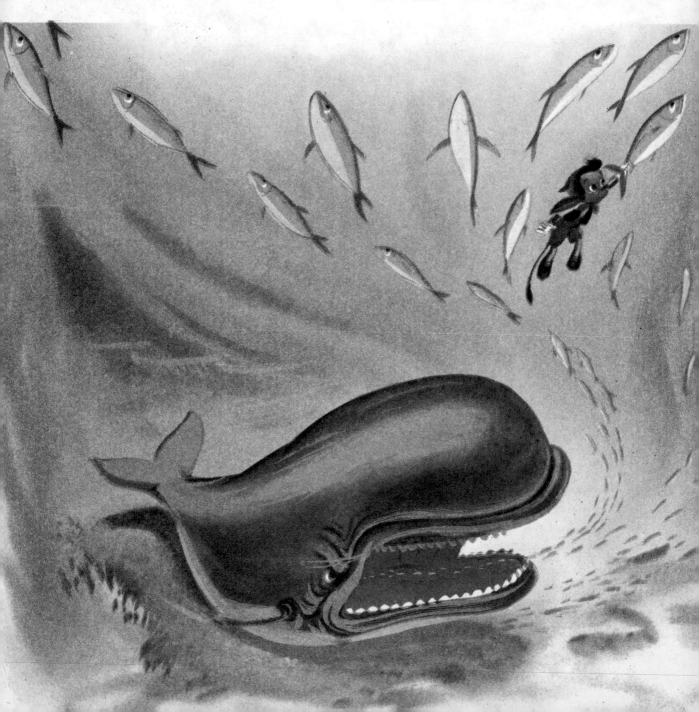

When Monstro woke, opened his eyes and saw the school of tuna approaching, he threshed the ocean into turmoil for miles around.

Pinocchio noticed every creature in the sea taking flight, but he did not understand the reason until he saw the whale coming toward him. Then he *knew*.

"Monstro!" he shrieked. "Jiminy, swim for your life!" For although he had long been in search of the Terror of the Deep, a mere look at those crushing jaws was enough to make him flee in terror.

But nothing in Monstro's path could escape. He swallowed hundreds of tuna at one gulp. Into that huge maw finally went Pinocchio!

At last, completely satisfied, the whale grunted and settled down for another nap.

"Blubber-mouth!" cried a shrill, small voice. "Let me in!"

It was Jiminy, clinging to an empty bottle, bobbing up and down outside Monstro's jaws, begging to be swallowed too.

But the whale paid no attention, except to settle farther into the water. The little cricket was left alone, except for a flock of seagulls who began to swoop down and peck at him. He raised his umbrella and drove them away, got inside the bottle and prepared to wait for Pinocchio.

Inside the whale, although Geppetto's bin was already heaped, he was still at work pulling in tuna.

"There's enough food to last us for months," he told Figaro joyfully. "Wait, there's another big one!" He scarcely noticed a shrill little cry of "Father!"

"Pinocchio?" the old man asked himself in wonderment, and rubbed his eyes. There, standing before him, was his boy! "Pinocchio!" he exclaimed joyfully. "Are my eyes telling me the truth? Are you really my own dear Pinocchio?"

Geppetto was not the only one who was glad. Figaro licked Pinocchio's face, and little Cleo turned somersaults.

"You see, we have all missed you," said Geppetto fondly. "But you're sneezing! You've caught cold, son! You should not have come down here! Sit down and rest! Give me your hat!"

But when Pinocchio's hat was removed, those hated donkey ears popped out into plain sight.

"Pinocchio!" cried Geppetto, shocked. *"Those ears!"*

Pinocchio hung his head in shame. "I've got a tail, too," he admitted sadly. *"Oh, Father!"* And he turned his head away to hide his tears.

"Never mind, son," Geppetto comforted

him. "The main thing is that we are all to-gether again."

Pinocchio brightened up. "The *main* thing is to figure out a way to get out!"

"I've tried everything," said Geppetto hopelessly. "I even built a raft—"

"That's it!" cried Pinocchio. "When he opens his mouth, we'll float out on the raft!"

"Oh, no," argued Geppetto. "When he opens his mouth everything comes in—nothing goes out. Come, we are all hungry—I will cook a fish dinner! Help me build a fire—"

"That's it, Father!" interrupted Pinocchio. "We'll build a great big fire!" And he began to throw into the fire everything he could get his hands on.

"Not the chairs!" warned Geppetto. "What will we sit on?"

"We won't need chairs," shouted Pinocchio. "We'll build a big fire and make Monstro sneeze! When he sneezes, out we go! Hurry—more wood!"

As the fire began to smoke they got the raft ready.

"It won't work, son," Geppetto insisted mournfully.

But before long the whale began to grunt and cough. Suddenly he drew in his breath and gave a monstrous SNEEZE! Out went the raft, past those crushing jaws, into the sea.

"We made it!" shouted Pinocchio. "Father, we're free!"

But they were not yet free. The angry whale saw them and plunged ferociously after their frail raft. He hit it squarely, splintering it into thousands of pieces. Pinocchio and Geppetto swam for their lives, with Monstro, the Terror of the Deep, in full pursuit.

The old man clung weakly to a board. He knew he could never reach land, but there was still hope for Pinocchio.

"Save yourself, my boy!" cried Geppetto. "Swim for shore, and don't worry about me!"

But the brave puppet swam to his father and managed to keep him afloat. Giant waves swept them toward the dark, forbidding rocks which lined the shore. Even if they escaped Monstro, they would surely be crushed to death.

But between two of the rocks there was a small, hidden crevice. By some miracle, Pinocchio and Geppetto were washed through this crevice into a small, sheltered lagoon. Again and again the furious whale threw his bulk against the rocks on the other side. His quarry had escaped!

But alas, when Geppetto sat up dizzily he saw poor Pinocchio lying motionless beside him, still and pale. The heartbroken old man knelt and wept bitterly, certain his wooden boy was dead.

The gentle waves carried a fishbowl up onto the beach. It was Cleo—and to the edge of the bowl clung a bedraggled kitten, Figaro. But even they were no comfort to Geppetto now.

A bottle bobbed up out of the water. Inside it rode Jiminy Cricket. He saw what had happened and longed to comfort Geppetto, but his own heart was broken.

The sorrowful old man finally gathered poor Pinocchio in his arms, picked up his pets and started home. They too felt sad, for they knew Geppetto was lonelier than he had ever been before.

When they reached home, it no longer seemed a home; it was dark and cheerless. Geppetto put Pinocchio on the workbench, buried his face in his hands and prayed.

Suddenly a ray of starlight pierced the gloom. It sought out the lifeless figure of the puppet. A voice which seemed to come from the sky said, as it had said once before:

"—and some day, when you have proven yourself brave, truthful and unselfish, you will be a real boy—"

The old man saw and heard nothing. But Pinocchio stirred, sat up and looked around. He saw the others grieving, and wondered why. Then he looked down at himself, felt of his arms and legs, and suddenly he realized what had happened.

"Father!" he cried. "Father, look at me!"

Pinocchio was alive—really alive. No longer a wooden puppet, but a real flesh-and-blood boy!

Geppetto stared unbelievingly. Once more he picked Pinocchio up in his arms and hugged him, and cried—this time for joy. Again a miracle had been performed; this was truly the answer to his wish—the son he had always wanted!

What did they do to celebrate? Geppetto made a fire and soon the house was as warm and cozy as ever. He started all the clocks and played the music box. Figaro turned somersaults, and Cleo raced madly about her bowl. Pinocchio flew to get his precious toys; even they seemed gayer than ever.

As for Jiminy Cricket, he was the happiest and proudest of all. For on his lapel he now wore a beautiful badge of shining gold!

PETER AND THE WOLF

Far up in the north of Russia, in a cozy cottage at the edge of a great forest, Peter lived with his grandfather.

Peter loved the forest. In summer he roamed its shady paths, visiting his friends the wild animals and birds. He loved the forest in winter, too, when a thick blanket of white snow covered the ground and the frozen lake and clung to the top-most branches of the trees. But in winter Peter could not go into the forest.

"Hungry wolves roam about in the winter," his grandfather told him when he caught Peter trying to steal out. "You must wait until you are old enough to hunt them."

But Peter was certain he was old enough for anything—and too smart for any wolf—right now! So he waited his chance, and when his grandfather dozed, off went Peter, armed with a coil of rope and his own little wooden gun. Down the path he went, ever so quietly, through the gate, across the snowy bridge and into the white forest.

At first Peter felt rather cold and lonely, with whiteness and silence on every side.

Then "Hello, Peter!" twittered a little voice like a flute, and down flew his old friend Sasha, the bird. "What are you doing alone in the forest in the winter?" asked Sasha.

"I'm out to hunt the wolf," said Peter stoutly. "Want to come along?"

Sasha did want to, so on they went together.

Suddenly, on the snowbank ahead, they saw a great threatening shadow. Could it be the wolf?

As Peter and Sasha stood there, quaking, the shadow moved toward them, and out from behind a tree stepped—another old friend of the summer, Sonia, the duck.

"Hello, Sonia," grinned Peter. "We're out to hunt the wolf."

"Oh," said Sonia, "may I come along?"

Of course, Peter and Sasha were glad to have Sonia with them, so she fell into line as they started on again.

But now as they marched along a slinking figure followed them, hidden among the reeds. It was Ivan, the sly cat, who kept hungry eyes on Sonia and Sasha.

As they reached a clearing, pounce! out jumped the cat and sprang at the bird. Only Peter's quick leap saved Sasha from Ivan's jaws.

Peter was shocked.

"Why, Ivan!" he said. "You're a bully!"

Ivan dropped his head guiltily.

"Come on, Sasha," said Peter. "Ivan is sorry. He won't do it again."

With a doubtful glance at Ivan, Sasha hopped back into line.

Once again the brave hunters marched on.

Suddenly, crunch! a lump of snow broke noisily behind them. The line of little hunters spun about.

There was the wolf!

Peter made the leap of his life to a low tree branch. Sasha fluttered up beside Peter on the low tree branch. Ivan scrambled up, too. But Sonia could not fly!

From their hiding places Peter and Sasha and Ivan anxiously watched Sonia scuttle across the snow with the wolf's breath hot upon her. Sonia disappeared from sight behind a fallen log, and they waited, breathless with suspense.

Then the wolf reappeared. And there were duck feathers clinging to his jaws.

Poor Sonia! Poor Sonia! But there was little time for sadness, for the wolf was snarling below Peter, Ivan, and Sasha.

A plan came to Peter! He whispered it to Sasha and Ivan, who twittered and purred their agreement.

First, Sasha flew down from his perch, and flew back and forth in the face of the wolf until the beast was frantic.

Then, down Peter's rope crawled Ivan the cat. Inch by inch Ivan moved closer to where the wolf was battling Sasha.

Ivan crept up behind the angry wolf, with the loop of rope ready for action. Down

went the rope over the wolf's tail! Zing! Ivan pulled the loop tight and Peter, on the bough above, pulled in the slack.

Soon the wolf felt the rope's pull. He reared around, snarling with fresh rage. But Ivan was back on the branch beside Peter, and they were both tugging. They were tugging with every bit of their strength.

There they were, Peter and Ivan, up on their tree branch, and there was the wolf snarling and snapping as he swung by his tail in mid-air.

Now it was Sasha's turn to fly into action again. For off in the forest sounded a hunter's horn. With a tweet of encouragement to his friends, Sasha flew off toward the sound. In and out among the branches he flew until below him he spied three stout hunters marching along.

What could the little bird do to make them follow him? He tried to imitate a wolf howl.

He sputtered and he chirped. Still the hunters did not understand.

"Something must be wrong," said one.

"This little fellow is trying to tell us something," agreed the second.

"Let us take a look," said the third.

So they followed Sasha back to the tree. But what was this? The wolf was snugly bound with the rope, and Peter and Ivan were sitting on him, swinging to and fro.

And who was that coming out from behind the log? It was Sonia, safe and sound, though still a little wobbly on her feet.

And what a gay parade as they entered

the village—Sasha and Ivan and Sonia, and the three hunters carrying the wolf. And at the head of them all, Peter marched proud- ly. Now even his grandfather had to be impressed. For Peter the hunter and his friends had captured the wolf!

GRANDPA BUNNY

DEEP IN THE WOODS where the brier bushes grow, lies Bunnyville, a busy little bunny rabbit town.

And in the very center of that busy little town stands a cottage, a neat twig cottage, with a neat brown roof, which is known to all as the very own home of Great Grandpa Bunny Bunny.

Great Grandpa Bunny Bunny, as every bunny knows, was the ancestral founder of the town, which is a very fine thing to be.

He liked to tell the young bunnies who always gathered around how he and Mrs. Bunny Bunny, when they were very young, had found that very brier patch and built themselves that very same little twig house.

It was a happy life they lived there, deep in the woods, bringing up their bunny family in that little house of twigs.

And of course Daddy Bunny Bunny, as he was called then, was busy at his job, decorating Easter eggs.

As the children grew up, they helped paint Easter eggs. And soon the children were all grown up, with families of their own. And they built a ring of houses all around their parents' home.

By and by they had a town there, and they called it Bunnyville.

Now Grandpa Bunny Bunny had lots of help painting Easter eggs—so much that he began to look for other jobs to do.

He taught some of the young folks to paint flowers in the woods.

They tried out some new shades of green on mosses and on ferns.

They made those woods so beautiful that people who went walking there marveled at the wonderful colors.

"The soil must be especially rich," they said, "or the rainfall especially wet."

And the bunnies would hear them and silently laugh. For they knew it was all their Grandpa Bunny Bunny's doing.

Years went by. Now there were still more families in Bunnyville. And Grandpa Bunny Bunny had grown to be Great Grandpa Bunny Bunny. For that is how things go. He still supervised all the Easter egg painting, and the work on the flowers every spring.

But he had *so* much help that between times he looked around for other jobs to do.

He taught some of the bunnies to paint the autumn leaves—purple for the gum trees, yellow for the elms, patterns in scarlet for the sugar maple trees. Through the woods they went with their brushes and their pails.

And the people who went walking there would say among themselves, "Never has there been such color in these woods. The nights, in these woods, must have been especially frosty."

And the bunnies would hear them and silently laugh. For they knew that it was all their Great Grandpa's plan.

And so it went, as the seasons rolled around. There were constantly more bunnies in that busy Bunnyville.

And Great Grandpa was busy finding jobs for them to do.

He taught them in winter to paint shadows on the snow and pictures in frost on wintry window panes and to polish up the diamond lights on glittering icicles.

And between times he told stories to each crop of bunny young, around the cozy fire in his neat little twig home. The bunny children loved him and his funny bunny tales. And they loved the new and different things he found for them to do.

But at last it did seem as if he'd thought of everything! He had crews of bunnies trained to paint the first tiny buds of spring.

He had teams who waited beside cocoons to touch up the wings of new butterflies.

Some specialized in beetles, some in creeping, crawling things.

They had painted up that whole wild wood till it sparkled and it gleamed.

And now, the bunnies wondered, what would he think of next? Well, Great Grandpa stayed at home a lot those days, and thought and thought. At last he told a secret to that season's bunny boys and girls.

"Children," Great Grandpa Bunny Bunny said, "I am going to go away. And I'll tell you what my next job will be, if you'll promise not to say."

So the bunny children promised. And Great Grandpa went away. The older bunnies missed him, and often they looked sad. But the bunny children only smiled and looked extremely wise. For they knew a secret they had promised not to tell.

Then one day a windy rainstorm pelted down on Bunnyville. Everyone scampered speedily home and stayed cozy and dry in the cottages.

After a while the rain slowed down to single dripping drops.

Then every front door opened, and out the bunny children ran.

"Oh, it's true!" those bunnies shouted. And they did a bunny dance. "Great Grandpa Bunny Bunny has been at work again. Come see what he has done!"

And the people walking out that day looked up in pleased surprise.

"Have you ever," they cried, "simply *ever* seen a sunset so gorgeously bright?"

The little bunnies heard them and they chuckled silently. For they knew that it was the secret. It was all Great Grandpa Bunny Bunny's plan.

BONGO

BONGO was a circus bear, a smart and lively circus bear. He was the smartest little bear any circus ever had. Yes, Bongo was the star of the show!

When the drums went tr-r-rum, and the bugles shouted, that was the signal for Bongo's act. Then the spotlights all pointed their long fingers of light down at an opening in the tent, and in rode Bongo!

In rode Bongo on his shiny unicycle, all aglitter under the glare of the lights. And his act began.

81

He juggled and danced on the highest trapeze. He walked a tightrope with the greatest of ease. Then up, up, up to the top of the tent went Bongo. And when he'd gone so high that he couldn't go higher, he rode his unicycle daringly on the high tight wire!

"Hurray for Bongo!" he heard voices call below.

"You know, he's the star who makes the show!"

Bongo was king of the circus while his act was on!

But when it was over, and Bongo the star rode out of the ring to the roar of applause, then clang went an iron collar around his neck. Rattle went a long chain as Bongo was led away to his boxcar. Slam went the barred door as it locked behind him. There sat Bongo, the star of the circus, just a bear in a gilded cage.

Poor Bongo! Oh, he was well enough treated. He was fed only the finest selected bear food, from his own tin dishes. He always had fresh water to drink. He was washed and combed and curried and clipped, and kept in the very finest condition.

But after all was said and done, he was still just a slave. He was lonely, too. And from somewhere deep in his past, the voice of the wild called to him.

"Bongo, Bongo, yoo-hoo, Bongo!" it sang.

He heard it in the scream of the train whistle, as the circus moved from town to town. He heard it in the clatter of the speeding wheels.

Each time the circus stopped in a new town Bongo went through his act as though he were in a dream. And when he was put back into his cage he lived in that dream—a dream of the wide-open spaces.

The voice of the wild kept calling, "Bongo!"

One day that call got into his blood so that he could not sit still. He paced around his cage as it jolted with the motion of the train. He shook the bars. He hammered at the door. And the boxcar door swung open!

Bongo was face to face with the great out-of-doors.

The train was moving slowly around a curve. Quickly Bongo swung out on his little cycle, dropped to the roadbed, and zipped away down a long hillside.

Behind him in the distance the train whistle faded, the hurrying cars disappeared from sight. And Bongo at last was free!

On down the hillside he sped, and into the woods he had dreamed of for so long. Bongo was wide-eyed at the wonder of this new world. For the trees towered taller than circus tent poles. The flowers were brighter than colored balloons. The crisp air smelled better than popcorn and fresh-roasted peanuts. It was wonderful!

"Yes, sir, this is the life for me!" said Bongo.

He felt so good that he just had to run and jump and sniff and snort. He even tried to climb a tree, but, plunk! down he came, flat on his back.

Poor Bongo—he had never even seen a tree before, except through the windows of the circus train.

"Well," said Bongo, "I guess that takes a little practice!"

He backed away again, and took another little run. And plunk! Down he fell!

Now the branches above him were filled with twitterings and chatterings. The little woodland animals had all come out to meet Bongo.

"Hello," said Bongo shyly. "Let's be friends."

They taught him which were the most fragrant flowers to sniff. They showed him how to peek at his reflection in a quiet pool.

"I've never had so much fun," Bongo told them happily. "Your forest is wonderful."

And as the sun dropped behind the trees, Bongo looked up at the velvet sky twinkling with stars, while all around him stretched the sleepy quiet of the woods.

"Yes, this is the life for me," Bongo yawned contentedly, as he curled up for a good sleep.

He dozed off, but soon he woke up with a start. The night, which had seemed so peaceful, was full of sounds. Far off somewhere a coyote howled. Just then a chilly gust of wind shivered through the forest.

"Maybe this wood is not the place for me after all," he thought lonesomely.

Then storm clouds blotted out the stars. Across the inky blackness, yellow lightning flashed, and thunder rumbled angrily. Cold, soaking rain poured down on poor Bongo.

"I wish I'd never left the circus," he thought. At last, though, the rain did stop. The clouds parted, and a friendly moon shone through. And Bongo slept.

He woke up next morning, stiff as a board and cranky as an old bear—and hungry! He tried picking berries, but they were not very filling. Then he tried fishing, but the fish all got away.

At last he turned from the pool with a discouraged sigh. But what was this?

Right before his very eyes Bongo saw another little bear. And the bear was smiling at him!

For a moment Bongo thought he must be dreaming. He pinched himself, but the little bear was still there. So Bongo scampered over to get acquainted.

"Hello," he said shyly. "My name is Bongo." And he tipped his little circus cap.

"My name is Lulubelle," said the other little bear. "Let's play something."

This was wonderful. For the first time in his life Bongo had a playmate! Off they went through the woods together.

Bongo was so busy thinking how happy he

was that he didn't pay much attention to the crashing of underbrush and the crunching of stones as Lumpjaw, the biggest, toughest bear in the forest, came stamping out.

"H-hello," said Bongo shyly. Perhaps this was another playmate, he thought.

Lumpjaw did not bother to speak. He just swung one great paw at the little bear, and bong! Bongo crashed against a tree trunk, headfirst! As he pulled himself to his feet and shook his dizzy head, Lumpjaw lunged forward to hit him again.

But Bongo's new friend stepped between them. While Lumpjaw fumed, she stepped up to Bongo—and slapped him soundly on the cheek.

Bongo couldn't believe it. But it was true enough. So that there could be no mistake, the bear he thought his friend slapped him on the other cheek.

Bongo's heart was broken. He turned and slowly rode away. He did not dream that when he did this, it hurt the feelings of his friend. For no one had ever told him the ways of bears. How could he know that when a bear likes another bear, he says it with a slap?

Off into the woods went Bongo, heartsick.

"I should never have left the circus," said Bongo to himself. "Nobody likes me here." And he sighed.

Soon, as Bongo rode along, he heard near by the pounding rhythm of heavy feet. It sounded as though they were dancing. And he heard deep voices rumbling in what sounded like a song.

Quietly Bongo crept to the edge of an open clearing. The clearing was full of bears, a double line of them. They were shuffling about in a clumsy bear dance, and singing a tuneless bear song, and exchanging clumsy bear slaps.

"Why, they're slapping each other," Bongo whispered to himself in surprise. "And they're not cross. They like each other!"

Then the words of the song reached him—

"Every pigeon likes to coo
When he says, 'I like you,'
But a bear likes to say it with a slap."

"With a slap!" cried Bongo. "Then Lulu-belle—she likes me! We're still friends!"

So Bongo raced out into the clearing, where his playmate was dancing with Lumpjaw, and gave her a sound slap.

Bongo's friend was delighted, but not Lumpjaw. He did not want any strange bear making friends with his playmate. He roared. He snorted. He fumed.. He chased Bongo through the forest, tearing up trees and hurling them at the little bear as he went.

Up the mountainside raced Bongo, with Lumpjaw close behind him. Down the other side Bongo hustled, while the great rocks Lumpjaw was hurling rolled past him.

Lumpjaw cornered Bongo at last, on the edge of a cliff. There they teetered and tottered and struggled and fought, until Cr-r-runch! Sw-w-wish! Spl-lash!

The rock beneath them crumbled away, and they tumbled down, down, down, into a roaring river.

Now the other bears gathered on the river bank far above to watch as Lumpjaw and Bongo rode the current on a twirling, plunging log.

Closer and closer they came to the great white-foaming falls. The watching bears all held their breath! Then over the falls tumbled the great log, with Lumpjaw still clinging to it! Over the falls and down the river went the log and the bear, until at last they floated out of sight!

And Bongo? All the bears shook their heads and sighed when they thought of him.

But wait! What was this? Up the steep river bank a wet little bear came climbing, with a dripping little circus cap still upon his head. Yes, it was Bongo, a tired Bongo, but a proud and happy little bear.

"I'm back," he told Lulubelle, and he said it with a real bear slap.

"I'm glad," said his friend, with a pat that knocked him down.

"This is the life," cried Bongo happily, as he scrambled back to his feet again. "This is more fun than the circus ever was. Yes, sir, this is the life for me!"

He felt so good that he juggled a handful of pine cones, and he did a little dance with a twisty twig for a cane.

Then his new friends showed him where to find the fattest, sweetest grubs to eat, and a honey tree running over with delicious honey. And they found him a cave that was dry and warm, and just right for him.

"This is the life," cried Bongo happily. And he threw his little old circus cap away, high up into the branches of a tree.

"Yes, sir," said he, "I'm Bongo the woods bear now!"

SNOW WHITE
AND THE SEVEN DWARFS

ONCE UPON A TIME in a far-away land, a lovely Queen sat by her window sewing. As she worked, she pricked her finger with her needle. Three drops of blood fell on the snow-white linen.

"How happy I would be if I had a little girl with lips as red as blood, skin as white as snow, and hair as black as ebony!" thought the Queen as she sewed.

When spring came, her wish was granted. But the Queen's happiness was very brief. As she held her lovely baby in her arms, the Queen whispered, "Little Snow White!" and then she died.

When the lonely King married again, his new Queen was beautiful. But, alas, she was also very heartless and cruel. She was very jealous of all the lovely ladies of the kingdom, but most jealous of all of the lovely little Princess, Snow White.

Now the Queen's most prized possession was her magic mirror. Every day she looked into it and asked:

"Mirror, mirror on the wall,
Who is the fairest of us all?"

If the magic mirror replied that she was the fairest in the kingdom, all was well. But if another lady was named, the Queen flew into a furious rage. She would summon her huntsman and have her killed.

As the years passed, Snow White grew more and more beautiful, and her sweet nature made everyone in the kingdom love her —everyone but the Queen.

The Queen's chief fear was that Snow White might grow to be the fairest in the land. So she banished the young Princess to the servants' quarters. She made Snow White dress in rags, and forced her to slave from morning to night.

But while she worked and lived in the servants' quarters, Snow White dreamed dreams of a handsome Prince who would come some day and carry her off to his castle in the clouds. And as she dusted and scrubbed—and dreamed—Snow White grew more beautiful day by day.

At last came the day the Queen had been dreading. She asked:

"Mirror, mirror on the wall,
Who is the fairest of us all?"

and the mirror replied:

"Her lips blood red, her hair like night,
Her skin like snow, her name—
Snow White!"

The Queen's face grew pale with anger. The Queen rushed from the room and called her huntsman to her.

"Take Princess Snow White into the forest and bring me back her heart in this jeweled box," she said.

The huntsman bowed his head in grief. He had no choice but to obey the cruel Queen's commands.

Snow White had no fear of the kindly huntsman. She went happily into the forest with him. It was beautiful there among the trees, and the Princess, not knowing what was in store for her, skipped along beside the huntsman, now stopping to pick violets, now singing a happy tune.

The huntsman watched Snow White as she skipped and sang through the forest. At last the poor huntsman could bear it no longer. He fell to his knees before the Princess.

"I cannot kill you, Princess," he said, "even though it is the Queen's command. Run into the forest and hide, but you must never return to the castle."

Then away went the huntsman. On his way back to the castle, he killed a small animal and took its heart in the jeweled box to the wicked Queen.

Alone in the forest, Snow White wept with fright. Deeper and deeper into the woods she ran, half blinded by tears. It seemed to her that roots of trees reached up to trip her feet, that branches reached out to clutch at her dress as she passed.

At last, weak with terror, Snow White fell to the ground. As the sun began to set, she lay there, sobbing her heart out.

Ever so quietly, out from burrows and nests and hollow trees, crept the little woodland animals. Bunnies and tiny chipmunks,

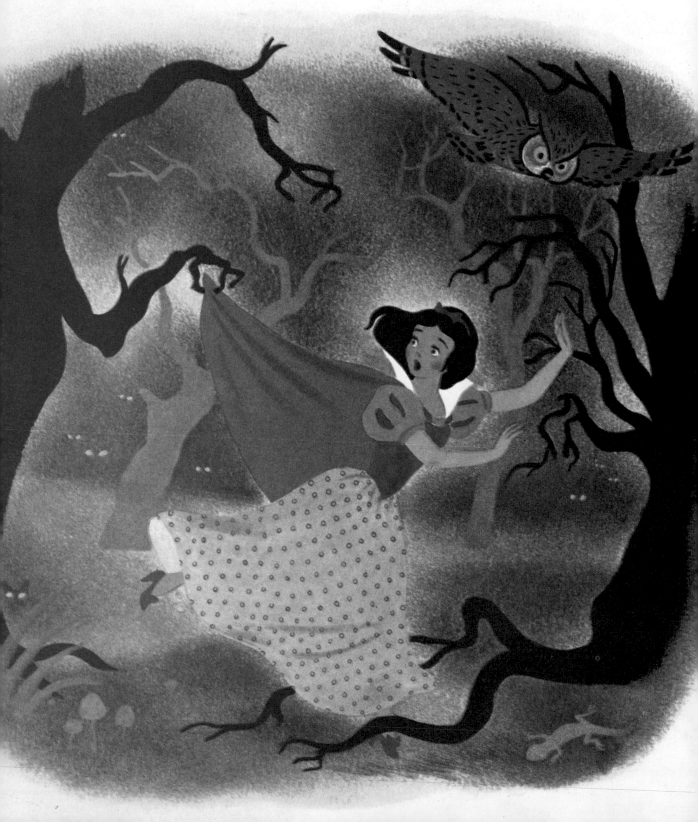

raccoons and squirrels, all gathered around. When Snow White looked up and saw them there, she smiled through her tears. At the sight of her smile, the little animals crept closer, snuggling in her lap or nestling in her arms. The birds sang their gayest melodies to Snow White, and the little forest clearing was filled with joy.

"I feel ever so much better now," Snow White told her new friends. "But I still do need a place to sleep."

One of the birds chirped something, and the little animals nodded in agreement. Then off flew the birds, leading the way. The rabbits,

chipmunks and squirrels followed after, and Snow White came with her arm around the neck of a gentle mother deer.

At last, through a tangle of brush, Snow White saw a tiny cottage which was nestled in a clearing up ahead.

"It's just like a doll's house," she cried.

Skipping across a little bridge to the house, Snow White peeked in through one window pane. There seemed to be no one at home, but the sink was piled high with cups and saucers and plates which looked as though they had never been washed. Dirty little shirts and wrinkled little trousers hung over chairs, and everything was blanketed with dust.

"Maybe the children who live here have no mother," said Snow White, "and need someone to take care of them. Let's clean their house and surprise them."

So in she went, followed by her forest friends. Snow White found an old broom in the corner and swept the floor.

Then Snow White washed all the crumpled little clothes, and set a big kettle of delicious soup to bubbling on the hearth.

"Now," she said to the animals, "let's see what is upstairs."

Up they all went. They found seven little beds all in a row.

"Why, they have their names carved on them," said Snow White. "Doc, Happy, Sneezy, Dopey—such funny names for children! Grumpy, Bashful, Sleepy! My, I'm a little sleepy myself!"

Yawning, Snow White sank down across the little beds and fell asleep. Quietly the little animals stole away, and the birds flew out the window. All was still in the tiny little house in the forest.

"Hi ho, hi ho,
    It's home from work we go—"

Seven little men came marching through the woods, singing on their way. As they came in sight of their cottage, they stopped short. Smoke was curling from the chimney, and the door was standing open!

"Look! Someone's in our house!"

"Maybe it's a ghost—or a goblin—or even a demon!"

"I knew it," said one of the little men with a grumpy look. "I've been warning you for two hundred years something awful was about to happen!"

At last, on timid tiptoe, in they went.

"Someone's stolen our dishes," growled the grumpy one.

"No, they're hidden in the cupboard," said Happy, with a grin. "But hey! My cup's been washed! Sugar's all gone!"

At that moment a sound came from upstairs. It was Snow White yawning.

"It's up there—the goblin—er demon—er ghost!" said one of the scared little men.

Shouldering their pick axes, up the stairs they went—seven frightened little dwarfs.

The seven little men stood in a row at the foot of their beds. They all stared at the sleeping Snow White.

"Wh-what is it?" whispered one. "It's mighty purty," said another. "Why, bless my soul, I think it's a girl!" said a third. And then Snow White woke up.

"Why, you're not children," she exclaimed. "You're little men. Let me see if I can guess your names."

And she did—Doc and Bashful, Happy, Sleepy, and Sneezy, and last of all Dopey and Grumpy, too.

"Supper is not quite ready," said Snow White. "You'll have just enough time to wash and change your clothes."

"Wash!" cried the little men with horror in their tones. They hadn't washed for oh, it seemed hundreds of years. But out they marched, when Snow White insisted. And it was worth it in the end. For such a supper they had never tasted. Nor had they ever had such an evening of fun. All the forest folk gathered around the cottage windows to watch them play and dance and sing.

Back at the castle, the huntsman had presented to the wicked Queen the box which, she thought, held Snow White's heart.

"Ah ha!" she gloated. "At last!" And down the castle corridors she hurried straight to her magic mirror. Then she asked:

"Now, magic mirror on the wall,
Who is the fairest one of all?"

But the honest mirror replied:

"With the seven dwarfs will spend the night
The fairest in the land, Snow White."

Then the Queen realized that the huntsman had tricked her. She flung the jeweled box at the mirror, shattering the glass into a thousand pieces. Then, shaking with rage, the Queen hurried down to a dark cave below the palace where she worked her Black Magic.

First she disguised herself as a toothless old woman dressed in tattered rags. Then she searched her books of magic spells for a horrid spell to work on Snow White.

"What shall it be?" she muttered to herself. "The poisoned apple, the Sleeping Death? Perfect!"

In a great kettle she stirred up a poison brew. Then she dipped an apple into it—one, two, three—and the apple came out a beautiful rosy red, the most tempting apple you could hope to see.

Cackling with wicked pleasure, the Queen dropped her poisoned apple into a basket of fruit and started on her journey to the home of the seven dwarfs.

She felt certain that her plan would succeed, for the magic spell of the Sleeping Death could be broken only by Love's First Kiss. The Queen was certain no lover would find Snow White, asleep in the forest.

It was morning when the Queen reached the great forest, close to the dwarf's cottage. From her hiding place she saw Snow White saying good-bye to the seven little men as they marched off to work.

"Now be careful!" they warned her. "Watch out for the Queen."

But when the poor, ragged old woman
with a basket of apples appeared outside her
window, Snow White never thought to be
afraid. She gave the old woman a drink of
water and spoke to her kindly.

SNOW WHITE AND THE SEVEN DWARFS   123

Thank you, my dear," the Queen cackled. "Now in return won't you have one of my beautiful apples?" And she held out to Snow White the poisoned fruit.

Down swooped the little birds and animals on the wicked Queen.

"Stop it!" Snow White cried. "Shame on you." The she took the poisoned apple and bit into it, and fell down lifeless on the cottage floor.

Away went the frantic birds and woodland animals into the woods to warn the seven dwarfs. Now the dwarfs had decided not to do their regular jobs that day. They were hard at work, making a gift for Snow White, to tell her of their love.

The seven little dwarfs looked up in surprise as the birds and animals crowded
around them. At first they did not understand. Then they realized that Snow White
must be in danger. "The Queen!" they cried,
and they ran for home.

The little men were too late. They came
racing into the clearing just in time to see
the Queen slide away into the shadows.
They chased her through the gloomy woods
until she plunged into a bottomless gulf and
disappeared forever.

When the dwarfs came home, they found Snow White lying as if asleep. They built her a bed of crystal and gold, and set it up in the forest. There they kept watch, night and day, hoping she might awake.

After a time a handsome Prince of a near-by kingdom heard travelers tell of the lovely Princess asleep in the forest, and he rode there to see her. At once he knew that he loved her truly, so he knelt beside her and kissed her lips.

At the touch of Love's First Kiss, Snow White awoke. There, bending over her, was the Prince of her dreams. Snow White knew that she loved him, too. She said good-bye to the seven dwarfs and, mounted on a white charger behind her Prince, rode off to his Castle of Dreams Come True.

DUMBO OF THE CIRCUS

THE CIRCUS ANIMALS paced back and forth in their cages nervously. They sniffed the air for the first smells of spring and peered at the skies anxiously.

Everyone in the circus was eager for spring to come. After long months at winter quarters in Florida, the clowns, the ringmaster, the musicians, the acrobats and the animal trainers were restless.

The trapeze artists were limbering up their muscles for their daredevil tricks. The circus train's locomotive, Casey Jr., was exercising his piston rods, and the calliope was practicing a few toots on his pipes. Before long, Casey Jr. would take the circus on tour.

They all stopped occasionally to look at the sky. They were expecting something!

Finally it came—a great flock of storks carrying big bundles in their beaks. The messenger birds zoomed low over the circus and dropped their packages. Parachutes blossomed forth, and the eagerly awaited bundles floated gently to earth.

When each bundle had been delivered safely, the circus animals were happy!

Leo Lion and his wife had four of the cutest cubs anyone had ever seen—

Mrs. Chimpanzee had a baby chimpanzee to dandle on her knees—

There was a tiny hippopotamus weighing only three hundred pounds—

An infant seal had come, as long as your hand and as bright as a cricket—

There was a baby tiger who loved to have his mother, Mrs. Tiger, polish his fur with her clean, soft tongue—

And two miniature zebras had come, complete with stripes—

But for Mrs. Jumbo, the elephant, who had been waiting so patiently, there was *nothing!* She scanned the sky for one of the messenger birds. As she waited, Mrs. Jumbo stamped nervously in her stall. Her elephant friends tried to comfort her, as much as possible. But it was difficult, for they were almost as disappointed as she was.

"Maybe the messenger's just a little late," one of the elephants said to Mrs. Jumbo. "Even a baby elephant is a heavy bundle for a stork, you know."

Mrs. Jumbo did not give up hope until the circus train pulled up on the loading platform and the animals marched into their cars. It was a happy time for everyone but the elephants. They did not want to go on tour without a baby elephant!

Casey Jr., the circus train locomotive, was not worrying about baby elephants. He blinked his lamps, stretched his piston rods to get the cramps out of them, blew the rust out of his whistle and a few experimental smoke rings out of his stack, and looked back to see how far the loading of the circus train had progressed. He whistled impatiently and shot a hiss of steam from his boiler to let everyone know he was ready.

"All aboard!" called the circus boss.

"All aboard!" whistled Casey, as he crouched low, pushed his wheels against the tracks, and pulled forward. The cars jerked into movement behind him, and he puffed away from the winter quarters, gaining speed and rolling along more and more easily.

Casey Jr. let out a long, high whistle. It was good to feel the cool fresh air rushing past him as he sped northward. He tooted a greeting to some birds who flew alongside him. He whistled to the cows in a field, who looked up and mooed to him, as they did every spring, when Casey Jr. passed.

As he rattled across the plains, the young colts in the pastures challenged him to races. Casey Jr. purposely slowed down to let them beat him in order not to hurt their feelings. This pleased the colts' mothers, who looked on proudly and decided that Casey Jr. was a grand fellow.

On and on the little locomotive chugged, tooting at steamboats when he ran alongside rivers, and at factories when he passed through cities. They whistled back, for they were all old friends of Casey Jr. Casey had serious responsibilities, too. In the mountains, when he saw a tunnel ahead, he had to toot a warning to the giraffes to pull their necks down. And there was one particularly long, dark tunnel where he wasn't exactly afraid, but it somehow kept up his courage to whistle to himself a little.

In the train behind him, clowns sang in time to the clickety-clack of the wheels, and the animals rocked their babies to sleep with the swaying motion of their cars. But in the elephant car, Mrs. Jumbo stayed alone in her compartment, and her friends stood together without chattering and gossiping as they usually did.

Mrs. Jumbo would have been much happier if she had known who was sitting on a cloud not far away.

It was a special delivery stork! He had detoured around a bad thunderstorm and had lost his way. But here he was at last, on the trail of Mrs. Jumbo. Far below, he could see the circus train crawling across the country.

"Look out below!" he cried, as he picked up his bundle and descended in a power dive.

"Mrs. Jumbo? Where's Mrs. Jumbo?" he called as he came up to the two giraffes, who pointed to the elephant car ahead.

"Oh, Mrs. Jumbo!" sang the stork.

"In here!" cried the elephants. "In here! This way, please!"

The stork flew through the opening in the roof into the car where Mrs. Jumbo was so eagerly waiting for him.

"Mrs. Jumbo?" the stork said, tipping his cap politely, and putting his bundle on the floor beside her.

Mrs. Jumbo started at once to untie it, but the messenger insisted that Mrs. Jumbo sign the receipt for one elephant before she opened the package. Then he tipped his hat and flew away, as all the other elephants gathered round excitedly.

"Quick, open the bundle, Mrs. Jumbo!" cried one of the elephants.

"I'm on pins and needles!" cooed another.

"This is a proud, proud day for us elephants," said a third.

And when Mrs. Jumbo's trembling trunk had at last unfastened the bundle, there lay a little elephant all curled up asleep.

"Isn't he a darling?" cooed one of the elephants to the others.

"Just too sweet for words," said another.

Mrs. Jumbo just beamed at the little fellow.

"What are you going to name him?" asked the first elephant.

"Little Jumbo," said the mother proudly.

"Kootchie, kootchie, kootchie!" went one elephant, as she tickled the baby playfully.

That made him sneeze! And when the baby sneezed, his ears, which had been hidden, flapped forward.

The elephants jumped back in amazement! Those were the most enormous ears anyone had ever seen on an elephant. They were larger by far than the ears on all the grown-up elephants! They could not help staring at the baby elephant. Even Mrs. Jumbo looked startled and amazed.

The baby elephant looked up and smiled. His ears dropped back down again and

dragged on the floor. One of the big elephants tittered.

"Isn't he silly looking?" she whispered to the elephant next to her, but in a whisper so loud that everyone heard.

"Simply ridiculous!" said the other. "Why, he's just a freak elephant, that's all."

Mrs. Jumbo glared at them, and beamed at her baby. When he grew into those ears he would be the biggest and most magnificent elephant in the world.

"I think you'd better change his name," said the oldest elephant, trying to make her voice sound especially sweet. "Jumbo won't quite fit, I think *Dumbo* is what you mean."

All the other elephants giggled and laughed merrily over this clever joke. But Mrs. Jumbo could stand it no longer. She slammed her compartment door in their faces.

Through the walls, the mother elephant heard the others laughing and joking. She lay down and took her little baby in her arms, caressing him gently with her trunk. The baby elephant made small contented noises and gradually fell asleep.

Everyone in the circus called the baby elephant Dumbo. His big ears became the great joke of the circus. Every time the train went through a tunnel, a clown said he hoped Dumbo had pulled his ears in first. When the wind blew strongly, the big elephants tried to act worried, saying that if the wind caught Dumbo's ears, it would pick up the whole train and blow it away.

Dumbo just smiled when he heard these things. He was just a little bewildered that others were not more friendly with him. He even laughed at some of the jokes himself. He thought that the idea of flying away in the wind was fine—it sounded like fun.

Mrs. Jumbo stayed in her own compartment almost all the time, and kept little Dumbo with her. Her temper grew worse, and she began to brood and worry. And it is not good for elephants to brood and worry.

An evening finally came when everyone forgot about Dumbo. That was when Casey Jr. puffed wearily to a stop in the city where the first show was to be given. It had been a long pull for Casey Jr., but despite his fatigue he was excited, too. Even the storm that was raging could not dampen the spirits of the members of the circus. They set to work in the driving rain to raise the tents and get everything ready for the first show, which was to be given the next day.

The roustabouts opened the doors of the freight cars and began to unload the tents and the ropes. The animal keepers led out the elephants and set them to work. The big animals lifted the tent poles in their trunks and carried them to the middle of the open lot. They pushed the circus wagons off the flat cars and pulled the heavy loads that men could not possibly handle. And all the time

they worked, the rain poured down on them and the thunder boomed.

When the lightning flashed, Dumbo could see short glimpses of the hurried work going on all around him. When the thunder rumbled he just grasped his mother's tail a little more firmly and kept on trudging behind her. Wherever she went, lifting, pulling, and hauling, he tagged along.

As the sun rose in the morning, the clouds were chased from the sky by a fresh wind, and the circus, all set and ready for the first show, glistened in the bright morning light.

After breakfast, everyone got ready for the big parade. The clowns put on their wigs and make-up and costumes. The horses were brushed until they shone, and bright ribbons were put on their manes and tails. The animals marched into their cage-wagons, and the elephants got in line, tail and trunk, tail and trunk. The calliope brought up the rear, his shining pipes uttering little toots of impatience. This first parade of the season was his first chance to play those tunes that delighted the children lining the streets.

Finally the parade began. Bright flags were flying and hundreds of cheering people lined the streets. Boys and girls, men and women, grandmothers and grandfathers and babies in their mother's arms, were all there, cheering as the beautiful white horses appeared at the head of the parade. Everyone cried with pleasure as the well-trained animals pranced and reared back gracefully.

Next came the first group of clowns, jumping and leaping and running in circles. Then the big cage-wagons with the wild animals rolled into view, followed by more clowns. In the distance people could hear the shrieking song of the calliope, and they knew that the end of the circus was approaching. But first came the elephants, marching majestically down the center of the street. They kept perfect step as they walked along, each elephant holding with his trunk the tail of the elephant in front of him. At the very end of the line came Dumbo. He had a hard time reaching up with his trunk to the tail of his mother in front of him. And he could not keep step, no matter how hard he tried.

At first glance people thought Dumbo was cute. But when they saw his floppy ears dragging on the ground, they tittered and giggled and some laughed out loud. The people laughed at Dumbo more than they had at the monkeys or the clowns. Monkeys and clowns are supposed to be laughed at, but elephants are dignified and majestic creatures. You can say "Oh!" or "Ah!" or "How big!" or "How strong!" about an elephant, but you just can't laugh at him.

Poor Mrs. Jumbo's ears burned to hear all the laughter over her little son. She glared furiously at the people on the sidewalks. She was glad when the parade was ended. But she did not know that even worse was in store for her and for Dumbo.

Back in the tent, Mrs. Jumbo gave Dumbo a bath so that he would look fine for the first show that afternoon. She scrubbed him with her trunk until he laughed and said it tickled. He splashed in his tub and made his own shower bath by taking water in his trunk and spouting it into the air over him.

When Mrs. Jumbo had carefully wrung out Dumbo's big ears and he had shaken himself dry, they ate their lunch and then went to their stalls in the menagerie. The other animals had taken their places, the performers were all ready, and the ringmaster had shined up his black top hat. Outside the big tent, the barkers were shouting to the first of the crowd, telling of the wonderful sights to be seen inside—the fat lady, the thin man, Stretcho the india-rubber man, the man who swallowed sharp swords, the man who ate fire, the lions, the tigers, the acrobats, the clowns, and the elephants.

Soon the crowd was streaming through the tents. A group of boys gathered near the rope in front of Mrs. Jumbo's stall. They pointed at Dumbo and laughed. Dumbo, trying to be friendly, walked toward them, but at the very first step he tripped on one ear and rolled on the ground. The little boys roared with laughter.

"What a wonderful sailboat he'd make," yelled one boy.

Another boy opened his coat and held it far out from his body.

"Look! Here's Dumbo!" he cried, as he wiggled his coat and everyone laughed.

Mrs. Jumbo could stand no more. She reached out quickly and grabbed one boy— who had just been sticking out his tongue at Dumbo. Then she spanked him soundly! The other boys screamed and ran away, and the keepers came running as fast as they could.

"Wild elephant!" someone yelled, and the crowd began to run for the exits.

When the first of the animals' keepers tried to push Mrs. Jumbo back into the corner of her stall, she picked him up with her trunk and tossed him into a pile of hay. The ringmaster came with a whip, and Mrs. Jumbo threw him into a big tub of water.

More keepers came running with their long, spiked poles. They poked Mrs. Jumbo, trying to force her back in her stall, where they could tie her fast. But now the mother elephant knew that they wanted to lock her up, away from her little Dumbo. She lifted her trunk and bellowed loudly. She knocked down the keepers in front of her.

But a man slipped behind her and quickly put a chain around her rear leg. Then other men rushed forward and bound her.

"Take her to the prison car!" cried the dripping ringmaster. "She's dangerous!"

So Mrs. Jumbo was led away to prison and Dumbo was left all alone. He didn't have anybody at all.

That night in the elephant tent, all the big animals were gathered around a pile of hay for dinner. They were busy eating and talking about the terrible things that had happened that day.

"I used to think he was funny," one of them said. "But now I think he's a disgrace. Mrs. Jumbo was a fine, decent, and respectable elephant until he came along."

"Dumbo is not just a disgrace to his mother," said another. "He's a disgrace to all elephants the world over."

On the other side of the pile of hay was a very tiny creature who listened wonderingly to their conversation. It was Timothy, the circus mouse. He had smoothed out a comfortable bed for himself, and was lying there wondering how soon he should step out and scare the elephants. As long as he lived, he never stopped getting a thrill out of scaring elephants. Whoever it was that arranged things so that elephants were frightened of mice had a great idea.

When Timothy was feeling a little blue, whenever he had a bad day—he could always make himself feel fine and important again just by scaring a bunch of elephants.

But today Timothy cocked his head on one side and listened carefully to the chatter of the big animals. Ordinarily the elephants didn't talk much while they were eating. Now they muttered and whispered in shocked tones, and Timothy guessed that they were really enjoying the whole affair even though they pretended to be horrified.

Something exciting had happened, anyway, Timothy concluded. Too bad he had missed it, whatever it was. It must have occurred while he was away searching for furniture for the new house he was building under the floor of the ringmaster's car. He stuck his head out of the hay to hear what the elephants were saying.

Then Dumbo came in, looking for something to eat. He smiled cheerfully up at the big elephants, for he was very lonesome. But when they saw him, they stopped talking at once, turned their backs on him, and closed the space around the pile of hay. The smile faded from Dumbo's face, tears came to his eyes, and he turned slowly away.

Now Timothy Mouse knew what the elephants were talking about. And when he saw Dumbo's ears he knew why.

"They can't do that to a little fellow," he muttered, "no matter who he is."

He brushed off his little red jacket, set his red bandmaster's cap at a jaunty angle, and leaped among the elephants.

"Boo!" he yelled, as loudly as he could.

The elephants jumped back, and looked at the tiny mouse with terror in their eyes. The tent became a mass of rushing elephants, bellowing, running, stamping, and squealing. One elephant ran up a ladder, and two of them even scurried up the tent poles. When

they were all just as far from the mouse as they could get, Timothy stood in the middle of the floor, put his hands on his hips, and glared around at them all.

"Pick on a little fellow, will you?" he cried. "You ought to be ashamed of your-selves! With all those big bodies you've got, you'd think there'd be a little heart in them. But no, not you! Just appetite and gossip, that's all. You wouldn't even let the little guy have something to eat. You made fun of him and called him names. You probably did the same thing to his mother and drove her wild. And why? Just because he was born a little different from you, that's all. Sure, I can figure it out. He's got big ears. So what of it? I'll bet he's got a heart inside of him, and that counts. It's more than you've got."

He paused for breath and looked around.

"Boo!" Timothy Mouse yelled again. "Boo! Boo! Get out of here!"

With a yell of fright, the terrified elephants dashed out of the tent.

Timothy knew it would be at least a half hour before they were all rounded up and brought back again. He smiled to himself and looked around for Dumbo.

"Hey, little fellow, where are you? Where are you, Dumbo?" he called.

Then he saw the tip of a little trunk waving from under a bale of hay. Timothy walked over and patted the trunk.

"No need to be afraid, Dumbo," he said. "Come on out. That's just an act I put on for those big fellows."

Dumbo had been afraid. But when he had listened to Timothy Mouse telling those great big elephants how mean they were, when he had heard the mouse telling them all it didn't make any difference just because he had big ears, Dumbo's heart had been warmed as never before.

"It's lucky for you I came along," said Timothy, "because I'm the one to help you out of your troubles. You leave all your troubles to Timothy Q. Mouse."

Dumbo crept out from under the pile of hay and stood beside Timothy Mouse, who looked him over very carefully.

"Pretty big ears, all right—" he said, almost to himself. But when he saw Dumbo look sad again he added, "But that's all right. No, it's better than all right. See, you're different from all other elephants. That's something. What if you were just like the rest of them? What would that get you? Not a thing. But you're different. You're a little elephant with big ears, so you ought to figure out something you can do that no other elephant can do. Then they'd all look up to you."

Timothy began to pace back and forth across the floor, thinking hard. Dumbo grabbed the mouse's tiny tail in his trunk and walked up and down behind him, just the way he did with his mother. Somehow, Dumbo felt safe and secure with Timothy.

"I've got it!" Timothy shouted, whirling around. "If you could just be a big success in the circus, they'd let your mother out of prison. And all the elephants would admire you, and so your mother would be happy and everything would be all right."

Dumbo nodded. Everything sounded so easy when Timothy talked about it.

"So we must figure out an act of some kind," Timothy muttered. "An act just made for you. Say—you know that big elephant balancing act right at the end of the performance?"

Dumbo nodded eagerly.

"Well," said Timothy, "just picture this. The elephants have finished building their pyramid. Then you rush out, with a flag in your trunk. See?"

Dumbo nodded again.

"You run across the ring," said Timothy Mouse, "to that springboard the acrobats use. Now remember Dumbo, the springboard is always pulled to one side of the ring before the elephant act. Well, you run and jump on the springboard and leap right up to the very top of that pile of elephants! Then you wave the flag! The audience applauds! and you're the hit of the show!"

Dumbo was very excited. But he shook his head wonderingly.

"Sure, you can do it!" cried Timothy. "I'll help you. We'll sneak out and practice at night for a while. We'll show 'em!"

With an affectionate pat on Dumbo's trunk he scampered away. Dumbo started eating the hay, paying no attention to the other elephants when they returned, still nervous and worried about the mouse. Dumbo smiled when he thought how his friend Timothy frightened them so much.

Later that night, Dumbo was sound asleep in his stall. He felt a tiny tapping against his trunk, and there was Timothy.

"Come on, Dumbo," he whispered. "We've got to practice the act."

It was not an easy job. Dumbo ran up to the springboard all right. He bounced on it hard and flew into the air. But then he lost all control. Sometimes he landed on his back, sometimes on his tail, sometimes on his trunk, sometimes on his head.

Once in a while Dumbo just bounced up and down on the springboard. He said that bouncing up and down made him feel as if he were flying. He would have liked to bounce up and down for hours, but Timothy always made him get back to work.

After several nights of practice, Dumbo improved. He could land on his feet, even when he jumped from the springboard to a stand ten feet high, then fifteen feet high, then twenty feet high.

Then Timothy decided Dumbo was ready for his big act. The next day, the performance went on as it always did. But little did the elephants or the ringmaster know what Timothy and Dumbo were planning.

Dumbo was as nervous as he could be. So much depended on his doing everything right. He clutched his little flag tightly.

The great moment finally came! The pyramid of balancing elephants was swaying in the ring. The audience was applauding loudly.

"Now!" cried Timothy.

Before he knew it, Dumbo was running toward the springboard.

THEN IT HAPPENED!

Dumbo tripped over his ears!

A gasp rose from the audience as Dumbo fell and rolled trunk over tail, trunk over tail straight for the springboard. He hurtled the length of the board, bounced into the air, and crashed right against the big ball on which the bottom elephant was balancing. The ball started to roll, and desperately the bottom elephant fought to control it while the pyramid above him swayed and rocked crazily in and out of balance.

"Run for you lives!" screamed someone in the audience, and there was a rush for the exits. Round and round, back and forth, the tottering mountain rolled. It crashed into circus apparatus, tore away ropes and poles, knocked the trapeze artists off their perches, and drove panicky clowns before it. The ringmaster tore his hair and jumped on his hat.

Little Dumbo, confused, dazed, and scarcely knowing what he was doing, stumbled after the reeling pyramid, waving his flag in his trunk with a pathetic hope that he might still get to the top.

But now the top elephant seized the center pole of the tent with his trunk. He clung to it even when it swayed and creaked and the ropes snapped. The great tent sagged and then, with a crash, the pole toppled to the ground and the whole structure gave way. Amid yells and screams and roars and bellows, the tent settled to the ground.

From the wreckage, the trunk of a little elephant waved a tiny flag.

It was night. Casey Jr. had pulled the circus train out of town far behind schedule because of the wreck caused by Dumbo's fall, which had disgraced the entire circus.

The elephant car looked like a hospital. Old Rajah stood with a sling supporting his heavily bandaged trunk. "Sixty years I've been in the circus," he moaned, "but never have I seen anything like that."

Another elephant with big lumps on his head cried, "Yes, and it was that ridiculous little son of Mrs. Jumbo that did it, too."

"He's a disgrace to our race," said another elephant. "I think we should disown him."

"Yes! You're right!" they all cried.

"It's a real shame," Old Rajah said to the elephants. "But I suppose it's the only thing to do. We can't ever admit to anyone that an elephant became a clown."

"A clown?" gasped others in horror.

"Yes, that's his punishment," Rajah said. "The ringmaster has decided to turn him over to the clowns."

The elephants all agreed that this was indeed the worst punishment that could have been found for an elephant.

At the next town the circus equipment was repaired and the clowns prepared for their new act with Dumbo. They fastened a bright yellow ruff around his neck. They powdered his head a clownish white, and on his sad face they painted a big crimson grin. A pointed dunce cap topped off the silly make-up.

Dumbo was the saddest little elephant in the whole world.

Oh, it was fine for the crowds, who had never seen anything so funny. It was fine for the ringmaster, who at last could figure on some profit from his ridiculous little elephant. It was fine for everyone but Dumbo, who cried himself to sleep every night, and for his mother, who wanted more than ever to be with her little son to comfort him and care for him, and for Timothy, who felt that it was really all his fault because his idea had turned out so badly.

Timothy tried to smile and make Dumbo feel good. He said he would have another idea, a better one that would surely work. But he knew the clowns would never let Dumbo go, that no one would ever give him a chance again.

The new act was the hit of the show. The clowns built, right in the middle of the big tent, a three-story building. Of course, it was only a false front, like a movie set. Suddenly flames and smoke belched from the windows and the clowns rushed in dressed like firemen. Their buckets were sieves and their hoses squirted just a drop of water at a time, and the audience roared at their antics.

Suddenly, at the topmost window, Dumbo appeared. Wearing a golden wig and dressed in a pink nightgown, he was frantically waving a white handkerchief in his trunk. A clown rushed into the tent—crying to the firemen to save her darling child. The fire fighters brought out a large round safety net and cried, "Jump! Jump!"

Then Dumbo jumped. Down, down, down he hurtled as the crowd howled in excitement. Dumbo hit the net hard—and crashed right through it, landing in a large tub of white plaster underneath.

The audience roared with laughter and the clowns took their bows. It was the biggest success of the circus!

Yes, Dumbo was now the great climax of a big success. But it brought him no happiness. He trudged out of the tent, dripping wet plaster behind him, having fun poked at him all the way. As he passed the other elephants they turned their backs to him, and even the monkeys looked the other way.

But back in his stall there was Timothy. Timothy was smiling bravely, telling Dumbo there was still a little plaster behind his ears as he washed himself, trying to make jokes and see Dumbo laugh. But it was no use. Dumbo wouldn't smile. He wouldn't eat, even when Timothy brought him a few peanuts he had saved for him.

Timothy did not know what to say as they settled down to sleep. He climbed up Dumbo's trunk and found a comfortable bed in the brim of Dumbo's little pointed hat.

"Dumbo," he said.

Dumbo just nodded slowly to show Timothy he was listening.

"Dumbo, I'm going to figure out something so that this clown business stops, so your mother will be free, and so you'll be a success. Now just go to sleep and stop worrying. Pretty soon you'll be a great success, you'll be happy, you'll be flying high!"

Dumbo smiled. Timothy was a good friend, even if his ideas didn't work. He dropped off to sleep, smiling over Timothy's idea that soon he would be flying high. That reminded him of the times he used to jump from the springboard. How good that felt!

Dumbo fell asleep, dreaming of that one great chance, which had turned into such failure, and now in his dream it became a great success. He waited at the entrance, sped gracefully toward the springboard, and bounced high into the air. Up and up he soared, gliding into the air with such ease that it seemed no effort at all.

It was a wonderful dream, and it seemed very real to Dumbo.

The morning sun rose on a perfectly natural landscape. There were trees and grass and a brook and a road. But there was something wrong about the scene. It was not at all according to Nature or Nature's laws that a certain tree should bear, high up in its branches, the form of a sleeping elephant.

The elephant was comfortably cradled in a forked limb, lying on its back with its ears and legs dangling loosely. The ears were unmistakable. It was Dumbo! And in the brim of his hat lay Timothy, still sleeping soundly.

A noisy group of birds had gathered around them, chattering their disapproval and scolding shrilly. Timothy stirred, disturbed by the insistent racket, and opened his eyes sleepily. He blinked, and a pair of eyes not a foot away blinked right back at him. A large, rusty-looking crow, evidently the leader of the birds, was glaring at him sternly. Timothy shifted uncomfortably.

"What are you doing down here?" he finally asked irritably.

"What are *you* doing up *here?*" the crow snapped back.

"Oh, go away!" said Timothy, who didn't like to be bothered before he was fully awake. He closed his eyes and settled down for another nap, since Dumbo was still asleep. "I'm here because I belong here," he muttered to the crow. "I live here!"

"So do we!" cawed the crow.

This made Timothy blink again.

"Oh, stop talking nonsense," Timothy said. "Run along and mind your own business."

"Haw!" cawed the crow loudly. "That's good! I suppose it's not my business when an elephant comes flying in here at midnight! And it's not my business when you knock my nest to pieces and scare my whole family out of their feather beds! Say, do you have any idea where you are?"

"Sure," replied Timothy, rubbing his eyes. "I'm right where I belong, in the circus. And what are you and your friends doing around this tent, I'd like to know."

Screams of laughter burst from the circle of birds. Timothy sat bolt upright and peered down to look at Dumbo, whose eyelids were beginning to flicker. Then he gazed at the canopy of leaves overhead, the trunk, the bark, and the branches of what certainly was a tree. And then he looked down—far, far down—at the ground.

They really *were* up in a tree!

"Dumbo!" he cried. "Dumbo! Take a look down—down there!" But just as Dumbo, who was still sprawled out on his back, started to turn his head, Timothy thought better of it. "NO, DON'T! DON'T LOOK!"

Dumbo had already glanced down. For one long minute he looked. Then he scrambled to his feet. Trying to balance in the wobbly fork of the tree, he teetered back and forth like a tightrope walker in a high wind.

Dumbo lost his hold and fell to the branch below. Timothy clutched the elephant's hat brim and shut his eyes. The second branch broke, and Dumbo fell. He clutched at the lowest branch, and it seemed that it might save him. But elephants were never meant to cling to branches. Dumbo fell!

He landed in a shallow brook that flowed under the tree, and Timothy fell into the water beside him. Dripping wet, the two sat in the stream while raucous shouts of laughter poured down on them.

"Now, try to keep your feet on the ground," cawed one crow. "It's not right for elephants to fly."

Dumbo and Timothy picked themselves up without a word and trudged off into the woods. They were bewildered and confused. Where were they? Dumbo could not imagine what had happened.

Timothy was speechless. He plodded along, hands clasped behind his back, his face a mask of puzzlement. Thoughts popped in his mind like firecrackers. "It's not right for elephants to fly? I wonder what that old crow meant. How did we ever get up into that tree? Dumbo can't fly. He hasn't got any wings. The only thing he has are those big—*say*, that gives me an idea!"

He stopped and turned to Dumbo. "Did you fly last night?"

Dumbo shook his head and smiled at Timothy as if he were a little crazy. Then he stopped with a startled expression.

"What is it?" Timothy asked impatiently. "Come on, tell me!"

Dumbo told Timothy Mouse about his dream the night before—how he had jumped on the springboard, sailed into the air, and flown away.

"If dreams could only come true, Dumbo!" Timothy said. "Well, I guess there's nothing to that flying idea."

They walked on aimlessly. But the same thought kept running through Timothy's head. "We got up into that tree somehow, dream or no dream. And people have walked in their sleep—so why couldn't they fly in their sleep?"

Timothy Mouse stopped and put his hands on his hips. "That just must be the answer! Dumbo flew in his sleep, and that's how we got up in that tree. And if Dumbo hasn't got wings, then the only thing he could fly with are his ears!"

He turned to Dumbo. "Listen, Dumbo. You can fly. You were right! You flew last night. You are going to fly again! Come on over here and we'll practice."

Dumbo followed Timothy obediently. But he remembered the many bad falls he had taken when he practiced on the springboard, and he remembered how that idea had finally turned out. This would be even worse. But he could think of nothing else to do, so he put himself in Timothy's hands.

In the field, they set to work. Timothy told Dumbo to flap his ears up and down vigorously, going faster and faster.

"One! Two! One! Two! Up! Down! Up! Down! Faster! Faster!" Timothy Mouse shouted at the little elephant.

Dumbo flapped his ears in time and a cloud of dust arose around them. Birds and small animals of the woods gathered around this strange sight in curious wonder. Then the flapping became slower and slower and ceased altogether, and out of the dust staggered the two grimy and choking partners.

From the trees around them came a chorus of laughs and jeers from their audience, chiefly from the crows who had followed them through the woods.

"Get a balloon!" shrieked the leader of the crows, and the others cackled loudly.

Timothy Mouse gritted his teeth, pulled his hat way down over his ears, and began with Dumbo again.

Dumbo galloped in a circle, and about every fifth step his flapping ears lifted him off the ground a few inches. The birds thought this was the funniest thing they'd ever seen, and they fluttered along beside him, imitating his clumsy efforts. Dumbo, confused and excited, didn't look where he was going and ran into a tree. He lay sprawled on the ground while the birds gathered round and jeered.

"Happy landings!" the big crow cackled, and the other crows cawed their approval. Even Dumbo thought it was funny, much to Timothy's disgust.

"Don't pay any attention to them," he said to Dumbo. "They probably laughed at the Wright brothers, too. You're doing fine. Now let's go over to this little hill and take off from there."

Dumbo took off from the little hill, all right, but he landed, too—in a mudhole. And Timothy, who made the trip in Dumbo's hat, bore his share of the crack-up.

The crows followed Timothy and Dumbo and laughed louder than ever.

Timothy could stand it no longer.

"Wait a minute!" Timothy shouted at them in a voice hoarse with rage.

The birds cocked their heads wonderingly.

"I want to ask you something. Is there a single one among you who has a heart?"

Timothy looked around at them all. The little mouse stared at them hard in the sudden silence. They all felt a little embarrassed.

"If there is," the mouse went on, more calmly, "I want to tell you a sad story. I want to tell you about somebody who had the misfortune of being born different from others—somebody who, just because he *was* different, and through no fault of his own, brought sorrow to himself and his poor old mother. This little fellow tried to hold his

head up and smile, to be a success. But then came the cruelest blow of all. They made him a CLOWN!"

A chorus of sympathetic noises came from the birds and animals.

Then Timothy drove home his point.

"Here I am trying to help my friend Dumbo be a success, and what do *you* do? You sit on your perches and laugh at us—yes, you laugh at us!"

The birds hung their heads guiltily. There was a silence, and then the big crow spoke.

"Well, you see," he said apologetically, "we didn't understand. We'll do whatever we can to help, won't we fellows?"

There was a loud cawing of approval as the birds flew down and gathered around Dumbo and Timothy.

The old crow took Timothy to one side. "Listen," he said, "the only reason Dumbo can't fly is that he hasn't any confidence. He just thinks he can't. We have the same trouble with our young ones. They don't want to try it at first, either. They're scared when they look out of the nest. So we give them a feather—any old feather—and tell them it's a magic feather from Persia and that anyone who holds it in his beak can fly. It always works. Here's a feather. Go on Timothy—try it on Dumbo."

Timothy took the feather from the old crow and ran joyfully back to Dumbo. The little elephant looked doubtful, but Timothy was so happy, so certain, so confident, that he began to believe him. When he took the feather in his trunk, he seemed to feel a new strength flowing into him.

Timothy climbed into Dumbo's hat, and the little elephant scampered up the hill once more. The birds gathered around expectantly, no longer making fun. There was silence as Dumbo stood on the crest of the hill and began to flap his ears. He closed his eyes, clutched the magic feather, and flapped his ears faster and faster.

Timothy held on to his hat. He closed his eyes to keep out the dust. He could not see a thing, but then he felt Dumbo moving beneath him. Then, as the dust cleared away, he looked over the brim of the hat. Dumbo was FLYING!

"Look, Dumbo, look!" Timothy shouted, and for the first time Dumbo opened his eyes. When he saw himself heading for a treetop, he almost fainted and fell, but he clutched the feather, flapped his ears, and banked gently in a curve around the tree. The crows flew around him, cheering encouragingly. Dumbo flew more and more gracefully, sailing through the air with ease.

It was wonderful! It was even more wonderful than his dream!

Slowly he leveled off to come to a landing. For his first attempt, it was pretty good. He bumped a little and nosed over on his trunk, spilling Timothy out on the ground. But the two partners did not mind at all. They got up laughing and shouting with glee as the birds circled around them, cawing their applause.

For the next few hours, Dumbo practiced. The crows taught him how to bank and turn and soar and glide and loop. In a short while Dumbo was making smooth three-point landings every time.

Timothy now saw that the sun was sinking; it was late.

"Say, we must be getting back to the circus," he said to Dumbo. "We're going to surprise them in that show tonight. We'll have to think of some story to explain where we've been all day."

The old crow told them how to get to the circus grounds, a few miles away, and with a dipping salute to his friends the crows, Dumbo flew away.

Timothy made him land on the edge of town and walk into the circus grounds. He had a carefully laid plan for the evening performance, and he didn't want Dumbo to give away their secret until exactly the right moment. Dumbo promised not to say a word.

And so the two partners came back home to the circus. Timothy scampered off to his house under the ringmaster's tent, and Dumbo brought joy to the clowns by his return. They had been afraid that the funny animal which was the climax of their act had disappeared forever.

Dumbo sat patiently while the clowns put on his make-up and his costume for the evening performance. And when the time came for him to climb up behind the window of the fake building, Timothy joined him and jumped into his hat.

"Our big moment has come, Dumbo!" Timothy whispered excitedly. "Just wait until after this act, and the whole world will be eating out of our hands."

Dumbo just nodded and smiled. Inside he was trembling, but he tried to act calm and serene. He didn't want Timothy to know that he was afraid. Dumbo looked confidently at the little black feather, which he clutched in the end of his trunk.

The clown act began. Smoke and flames poured from the windows of the building. The clowns rushed in with their sieve-buckets and waterless hoses. Dumbo stood at the window, the spotlight on him. Below he saw the clowns with the life-saving net spread out above the tub of wet plaster.

No more plaster for him! he thought. And he jumped. But at that moment, the black feather slipped from his trunk and floated away. Dumbo stared in horror, and his heart sank in fear. Was he to fail once again?

Timothy saw the feather go, too, and realized what effect this would have on Dumbo. As they plunged down, down, toward the ground, Timothy shouted to Dumbo, pleading with him to spread his ears and fly. But Dumbo seemed not to hear. He had closed his eyes and decided that once more his high hopes would be dashed. In a flash, Timothy jumped from the hat and holding on tightly, scampered down Dumbo's trunk and looked him in the eye.

"Dumbo!" he shouted frantically. "Dumbo! You *can* fly! That feather didn't mean a thing. It was fake. You can fly without it. You *can* fly! *You can fly!*"

Timothy's insistent words reached Dumbo's ears. He opened his eyes and saw the firemen's net just below him. "YOU CAN FLY!" screamed Timothy, as Dumbo spread his ears wide and swooped up into the air when he was not two feet above the net!

One mighty gasp arose from the great audience! They rubbed their eyes! They pinched themselves! They knew it couldn't be, but it was happening!

Dumbo was flying!

Timothy, who had braced himself for the crash, slowly opened his eyes and pulled himself back up to the hat brim. When he got his breath back, he looked over the edge and gloried in the sight of the wildly applauding crowd below him.

"Dumbo, you're wonderful!" he shouted. "Marvelous! The greatest thing on earth! Dumbo, look at them shouting for you! The audience is shouting for you, Dumbo!"

Dumbo swooped up to the highest point

in the tent and then plunged down, down, DOWN, and not until the very last instant did he level off and sail gently over the heads of the audience, which was in a state of utter collapse from the sheer excitement of it all.

Then Dumbo repeated his power dive. He flew upside down, barrel-rolled back to level flight, and did loops, spins, and falling leaves. He swooped down to pick up peanuts and squirted a trunkful of water on the clowns. The crowd roared.

The news spread like wildfire. The town was aroused and came rushing to the circus. All the animals in the circus, too, heard what was going on. And the animal keepers quickly brought Mrs. Jumbo from her prison car so she could watch her son thrilling the crowds. Dumbo dipped in salute to her as she came into the tent, and the crowd roared its applause for the mother of this flying marvel.

Dumbo flew for a full hour, and when he finally came to a beautiful landing by the

side of his mother, everyone was exhausted from the excitement, hoarse from shouting. With dignity, Dumbo escorted his mother to their stall, as Timothy held back the crowds that surged around.

"Stand back, everyone," he shouted. "Give the star a chance to rest. Give the great Dumbo, the Flying Elephant, an opportunity to have a little time alone with his dear mother. No conferences until tomorrow morning," cried Timothy Mouse.

And so Timothy became Dumbo's manager. And he saw to it that Dumbo got a wonderful contract, with a big salary, a pension for his mother, and a special streamlined car on the circus train. Dumbo flew in great aviation contests, made a good-will tour of South America, broke all altitude records, and helped the Army and Navy in their aviation training programs.

And through it all he remained the simple, kind little fellow that he had always been. He didn't forget his old friends the crows, who frequently went on private flying parties with him. He bought some shiny new whistles for Casey Jr. He saw to it that Timothy had always on hand a supply of every known type of cheese.

And now, as the circus train puffed across the country, Casey Jr. tooted his bright new whistles happily. In the elephant car, the big elephants stood on boxes, flapping their ears.

They jumped, hoping they would fly even a few feet. But each one of them crashed and gave up.

At last all the elephants, even Old Rajah, agreed that there could be only one Dumbo, the Flying Elephant.

In the special streamlined car at the rear of the train Dumbo sat snuggled close to his mother, Mrs. Jumbo, whose trunk was curled about him affectionately. Nearby sat Timothy Mouse contentedly humming a tune.

Thus the circus train with "Dumbo's Flying Circus" sped across the country toward the bright lights of Hollywood, where new triumphs awaited Timothy Mouse and Dumbo, the one and only Flying Elephant.

MOTHER GOOSE

JACK AND JILL

Jack and Jill went up the hill
   To fetch a pail of water.
Jack fell down and broke his crown
   And Jill came tumbling after.

Up Jack got, and home did trot
   As fast as he could caper,
Went to bed and plastered his head
   With vinegar and brown paper.

HICKETY, PICKETY

Hickety, pickety, my black hen,
She lays eggs for gentlemen;
Gentlemen come every day
To see what my black hen doth lay.

DING, DONG, BELL

Ding, dong, bell,
Pussy's in the well!
Who put her in?—
Little Johnny Green.
Who pulled her out?—
Big Johnny Stout.
What a naughty boy was that
To try to drown poor pussy cat,
Who never did him any harm,
But killed the mice in his father's barn.

A DILLAR, A DOLLAR

A dillar, a dollar,
A ten o'clock scholar,
What makes you come so soon?
You used to come at ten o'clock,
And now you come at noon.

OLD KING COLE

Old King Cole was a merry old soul,
  And a merry old soul was he;
He called for his pipes and he called for his bowl,
  And he called for his fiddlers three!

Every fiddler he had a fine fiddle,
  And a very fine fiddle had he;
Twee-tweedle-dee, tweedle-dee, went the fiddlers.
Oh, there's none so rare as can compare
  With King Cole and his fiddlers three!

159

CROSS PATCH

Cross patch,
Draw the latch,
Sit by the fire and spin;
Take a cup
And drink it up,
And call your neighbors in.

LITTLE BOY BLUE

Little Boy Blue, come blow your horn;
The sheep's in the meadow, the cow's in the corn.
Where's the boy that looks after the sheep?
He's under the haystack, fast asleep.

THE JOLLY MILLER

There was a jolly miller
   Lived on the river Dee;
He worked and sang from morn till night
   No lark so blithe as he.
And this the burden of his song
   Forever used to be—
"I care for nobody—no, not I,
   Since nobody cares for me."

DOCTOR FOSTER

Doctor Foster went to Gloucester,
    In a shower of rain;
He stepped in a puddle up to his middle,
    And never went there again.

LITTLE JACK HORNER

Little Jack Horner sat in a corner,
Eating a Christmas pie;
He put in his thumb, and took out a plum,
And said, "What a good boy am I!"

GEORGIE PORGIE

Georgie Porgie, pudding and pie,
Kissed the girls and made them cry.
When the boys came out to play
Georgie Porgie ran away.

THREE WISE MEN OF GOTHAM

Three wise men of Gotham
Went to sea in a bowl;
If the bowl had been stronger,
My song had been longer.

THE OLD WOMAN
WHO LIVED IN A SHOE

There was an old woman who lived in a shoe;
She had so many children she didn't know what to do.
She gave them some broth, without any bread;
She whipped them all soundly and sent them to bed.

SIMPLE SIMON

Simple Simon met a pieman,
   Going to the fair;
Says Simple Simon to the pieman,
   "Let me taste your ware."

Says the pieman to Simple Simon,
   "Show me first your penny."
Says Simple Simon to the pieman,
   "Indeed I have not any."

He went to catch a dickey-bird,
    And thought he could not fail,
Because he'd got a little salt
    To put upon his tail.

Simple Simon went a-fishing,
    For to catch a whale;
All the water he had got
    Was in his mother's pail.

He went for water in a sieve,
    But soon it all ran through;
And now poor Simple Simon
    Bids you all adieu.

LITTLE MISS MUFFET

Little Miss Muffet
Sat on a tuffet,
Eating her curds and whey.
There came a great spider,
And sat down beside her,
And frightened Miss Muffet away!

LITTLE
TOMMY TUCKER

Little Tommy Tucker
  Sings for his supper.
What shall he eat?
  White bread and butter.

How shall he cut it
  Without e'er a knife?
How shall he marry
  Without any wife?

RUB A DUB DUB

Rub a dub dub,
Three men in a tub,
And who do you think they be?
The butcher, the baker,
The candlestick maker.
Turn 'em out, knaves all three.

ROCK-A-BYE, BABY

Rock-a-bye, baby,
On the tree top!
When the wind blows,
The cradle will rock;
When the bough breaks,
The cradle will fall;
Down will come baby,
Cradle and all.

ONE TO TEN

1, 2, 3, 4, 5,
I caught a hare alive;
6, 7, 8, 9, 10,
I let him go again.

MISTRESS MARY

Mistress Mary, quite contrary,
How does your garden grow?
With silver bells and cockle shells
And pretty maids all in a row.

BAA, BAA, BLACK SHEEP

Baa, baa, black sheep, have you any wool?
Yes, sir, yes, sir, three bags full;
One for my master, one for my dame,
And one for the little boy who cries in the lane.

JACK BE NIMBLE

Jack be nimble,
Jack be quick,
Jack jump over
The candlestick.

WEE WILLIE WINKIE

Wee Willie Winkie runs through the town,
Upstairs and downstairs, in his night-gown;
Rapping at the window, crying at the lock,
"Are the babies in their beds, for now it's eight o'clock!"

BYE, BABY BUNTING

Bye, baby bunting,
Daddy's gone a-hunting,
To get a little rabbit's skin
To wrap the baby bunting in.

LITTLE BETTY BLUE

Little Betty Blue
    Lost her holiday shoe.
What shall little Betty do?
    Buy her another
To match the other,
    And then she'll walk in two.

JUMPING JOAN

Here am I, little Jumping Joan.
When nobody's with me,
I'm always alone.

DEEDLE, DEEDLE DUMPLING

Deedle, deedle dumpling, my son John,
Went to bed with his stockings on;
One shoe off and one shoe on,
Deedle, deedle dumpling, my son John.

PUSSY CAT, WHERE HAVE YOU BEEN?

"Pussy cat, pussy cat, where have you been?"
"I've been to London to look at the Queen."
"Pussy cat, pussy cat, what did you there?"
"I frightened a little mouse under her chair."

THIS LITTLE PIG

This little pig went to market,
This little pig stayed at home,
This little pig had roast beef,
This little pig had none,
This little pig cried, "Wee-wee-wee!"
All the way home.

RIDE A COCK HORSE

Ride a cock horse to Banbury Cross
To see a fine lady upon a white horse.
Rings on her fingers, and bells on her toes,
She shall have music wherever she goes.

PETER, PETER, PUMPKIN EATER

Peter, Peter, pumpkin-eater,
Had a wife and couldn't keep her;
He put her in a pumpkin shell,
And there he kept her very well.

MARY'S LAMB

Mary had a little lamb,
   Its fleece was white as snow;
And everywhere that Mary went,
   The lamb was sure to go.

It followed her to school one day;
   Which was against the rule;
It made the children laugh and play
   To see a lamb at school.

JACK SPRAT

Jack Sprat could eat no fat,
   His wife could eat no lean;
And so betwixt them both, you see,
   They licked the platter clean.

HARK, HARK

Hark, hark,
The dogs do bark,
The beggars are coming to town;
    Some in rags,
    Some in bags,
And some in velvet gowns.

HOT CROSS BUNS

Hot cross buns!
Hot cross buns!
One a penny, two a penny,
Hot cross buns!

If you have no daughters,
Give them to your sons.
One a penny, two a penny,
Hot cross buns!

IF I'D AS MUCH MONEY

If I'd as much money as I could spend,
I never would cry old chairs to mend,
Old chairs to mend, old chairs to mend—
I never would cry old chairs to mend.

If I'd as much money as I could tell,
I never would cry old clothes to sell,
Old clothes to sell, old clothes to sell—
I never would cry old clothes to sell.

HEY, DIDDLE, DIDDLE

Hey, diddle, diddle, the cat and the fiddle,
The cow jumped over the moon;
The little dog laughed to see such sport,
And the dish ran away with the spoon.

CURLY LOCKS

Curly Locks! Curly Locks! Wilt thou be mine?
Thou shalt not wash dishes, nor yet feed the swine,
But sit on a cushion and sew a fine seam,
And feed upon strawberries, sugar, and cream!

LITTLE TOMMY TITTLEMOUSE

Little Tommy Tittlemouse
Lived in a little house;
He caught fishes
In other men's ditches.

BOBBY SHAFTOE

Bobby Shaftoe's gone to sea,
Silver buckles at his knee;
He'll come back and marry me,—
Pretty Bobby Shaftoe!

THERE WERE TWO BLACKBIRDS

There were two blackbirds,
   Sitting on a hill,
The one named Jack,
   The other named Jill.

Fly away, Jack!
   Fly away, Jill!
Come again, Jack!
   Come again, Jill!

SING A SONG OF SIXPENCE

Sing a song of sixpence, a pocket full of rye,
Four and twenty blackbirds, baked in a pie;
When the pie was opened, the birds began to sing;
Wasn't that a dainty dish to set before the king?

The king was in the parlor, counting out his money,
The queen was in the kitchen, eating bread and honey;
The maid was in the garden, hanging out the clothes,
When along came a blackbird, and nipped off her nose.

PAT-A-CAKE

Pat-a-cake, pat-a-cake,
   Baker's man.
Bake me a cake,
   As fast as you can.
Pat it and prick it
   And mark it with Б.
Put it in the oven
   For Baby and me.

THERE WAS AN OLD WOMAN

There was an old woman tossed up in a basket,
   Seventeen times as high as the moon;
And where she was going, I couldn't but ask it,
   For in her hand she carried a broom.

"Old woman, old woman, old woman," said I,
   "O whither, O whither, O whither so high?"
"To sweep the cobwebs off the sky!"
   "Shall I go with you?" "Yes, by and by."

THE THREE
LITTLE PIGS

ONCE UPON A TIME there were three little
pigs who went out into the big world to
build their homes and seek their fortunes.

The first little pig did not like to work at
all. He quickly built himself a house of
straw. Then he danced down the road, to see
how his brothers were getting along.

The second little pig was building himself
a house, too. He did not like to work any
better than his brother. So the second little
pig decided to build a quick and easy house
of sticks.

Soon it was finished, too. It was not a very strong little house, but at least the work was done. Now the second little pig was free to do what he liked.

What he liked to do was to play his fiddle and dance. So while the first little pig tooted his flute, the second little pig sawed away on his fiddle, dancing as he played.

And as he danced he sang:

> "I built my house of sticks,
> I built my house of twigs.
> With a hey diddle-diddle
> I play on my fiddle,
> And dance all kinds of jigs."

Then off danced the two little pigs down the road together to see how their brother was getting along.

The third little pig was a sober little pig. He was building his house of bricks. He did not mind hard work, and he wanted a stout little, strong little house, for he knew that in the woods nearby there lived a big bad wolf who loved to eat up little pigs.

So slap, slosh, slap! Away he worked, laying bricks and smoothing mortar.

"Ha ha ha!" laughed the first little pig, when he saw his brother hard at work.

"Ho ho ho!" laughed the second little pig. "Come down and play with us!" he called to the third little pig.

But the busy little pig did not pause. Slap,

slosh, slap! Away he worked, laying bricks as he called down to his brothers:

"I build my house of stones.
I build my house of bricks.
I have no chance
To sing and dance,
For work and play don't mix."

THE THREE LITTLE PIGS   183

"Ho ho ho! Ha ha ha!" laughed the two lazy little pigs, dancing along to the tune of the fiddle and the flute.

"You can laugh and dance and sing," their busy brother called after them, "but I'll be safe and you'll be sorry when the wolf comes."

"Ha ha ha! Ho ho ho!" laughed the two little pigs again, and they disappeared into the woods singing a merry tune:

"Who's afraid of the big bad wolf,
The big bad wolf, the big bad wolf?
Who's afraid of the big bad wolf?
Tra la la la la-a-a-a!"

Just as the first pig reached his door, out of the woods popped the big bad wolf! The little pig squealed with fright.

"Little pig, little pig, let me come in!" cried the big bad wolf.

"Not by the hair on my chinny-chin-chin!" said the little pig.

"Then I'll huff and I'll puff and I'll blow your house in!" roared the wolf.

And he did. He blew the little straw house all to pieces!

Away raced the little pig to his brother's house of sticks. No sooner was he in the door, when knock, knock, knock! There was the big bad wolf! But of course, the little pigs would not let him come in.

"I'll fool them," said the wolf. He left the little pig's house, and he hid behind a tree.

Soon the door opened and the two little pigs peeked out. There was no wolf in sight.

"Ha ha ha! Ho ho ho!" laughed the two little pigs. "We fooled him."

Then they danced around the room, singing gaily:

"Who's afraid of the big bad wolf,
The big bad wolf, the big bad wolf?
Who's afraid of the big bad wolf?
Tra la la la la-a-a-a!"

Soon there came another knock at the door. It was the big bad wolf again, but he had covered himself with a sheepskin, and was curled up in a big basket, looking like a little lamb.

"Who's there?" called the second little pig.

"I'm a poor little sheep, with no place to sleep. Please open the door and let me in," said the big bad wolf in a sweet little voice.

The little pig peeked through a crack of the door, and he could see the wolf's big black paws and sharp fangs.

"Not by the hair of my chinny-chin-chin!"

"You can't fool us with that sheepskin!" said the second little pig.

"Then I'll huff, and I'll puff, and I'll blow your house in!" cried the angry old wolf.

So he huffed
  and he PUFFED
    and he puffed
      and he HUFFED,
and he blew the little twig house all to pieces!

Away raced the two little pigs, straight to the third little pig's house of bricks.

"Don't worry," said the third little pig to his two frightened little brothers. "You are safe here." Soon they were all singing gaily.

This made the wolf perfectly furious!

"Now by the hair of my chinny-chin-chin!" he roared. "I'll huff, and I'll puff, and I'll blow your house in!"

So the big bad wolf huffed and he PUFFED, and he puffed and he HUFFED, but he could not blow down that little house of bricks! How could he get in? At last he thought of the chimney!

So up he climbed, quietly. Then with a snarl, down he jumped—right into a kettle of boiling water!

With a yelp of pain he sprang straight up the chimney again, and raced away into the woods. The three little pigs never saw him again, and spent their time in the strong little brick house singing and dancing merrily.

CINDERELLA

ONCE UPON A TIME in a far-off land, there lived a kindly gentleman. He had a fine home and a lovely little daughter, and he gave her all that money could buy—a horse of her own, a funny puppy dog, and many beautiful dresses to wear.

But the little girl had no mother. She did wish for a mother and for other children to play with. So her father married a woman with two daughters. Now, with a new mother and sisters, he thought, his little daughter had everything to make her happy.

But alas! the kindly gentleman soon died. His fine home fell into disrepair. And his second wife was harsh and cold. She cared only for her own two ugly daughters. To her lovely stepdaughter she was cruel as cruel could be.

Everyone called the stepdaughter "Cinderella" now. For she had to work hard, she was dressed in rags, and she sat by the cinders to keep herself warm. Her horse grew old, locked up in the barn. And her dog was not allowed in the house.

But do you suppose Cinderella was sad? Not a bit! Cinderella made friends with the birds who flew to her window sill each day. Cinderella made friends with the barnyard chickens and geese. And her best friends of all were—guess who—the mice!

The musty old house was full of mice. Their homes were in the garret, where Cinderella lived. She made little clothes for them, and gave them all names. And they thought Cinderella was the sweetest and most beautiful girl in the world.

Every morning her friends the mice and birds woke Cinderella from her dreams. Then it was breakfast time for the household —with Cinderella doing all the work, of course. Out on the back steps she set a bowl of milk for the stepmother's disagreeable cat, who watched for his chance to catch the mice. The faithful dog had a tasty bone. There was grain for the chickens and ducks and geese. And Cinderella gave some grain to the mice—when they were out of reach of the cat. Then back into the house she went.

Up the stairway she carried breakfast trays for her stepmother and her two lazy stepsisters. And down she came with a basket of mending, some clothes to wash, and a long list of jobs to do for the day.

"Now let me see," her stepmother would say. "You can clean the large carpet in the main hall. And wash all the windows, upstairs and down. Scrub the terrace. Sweep the stairs—and then you may rest."

"Oh," said Cinderella. "Yes. I will finish all those jobs." And off to work she went.

Now across the town from Cinderella's home was the palace of the King. And in the King's study one day sat the King himself.

"The Prince must marry!" said the King to the Great Grand Duke. "It is high time!"

"But, Your Majesty, what can we do?" asked the duke. "First he must fall in love."

"We can arrange that," said the King. "We shall give a great ball, this very night, and invite every girl in the land!"

There was great excitement all through the land. And in Cinderella's home, the stepsisters were delighted, when the invitations to the King's ball arrived.

"How delightful!" they said to each other. "We are going to a ball at the palace!"

"And I—" said Cinderella, "I am invited to the ball, too!"

"Oh, you!" laughed the stepsisters.

"Yes, you!" mocked the stepmother. "Of course you may go, if you finish your work," she said. "And if you have something suitable to wear. I said IF, Cinderella." And she smiled a very horrid smile.

Cinderella worked as hard as she could, all through the long day. But when it was time to leave for the ball, Cinderella had not had a moment to fix herself up, or to give a thought to a dress to wear to the ball.

"Why, Cinderella, you are not ready. How can you go to the ball?" asked her stepmother, when the coach was at the door.

"No. I am not going," said Cinderella sadly.

"Not going! Oh, what a shame!" the stepmother said with her mocking smile. "But there will be other balls."

Poor Cinderella! She went to her room and sank sadly down, with her head in her hands.

But a twittering sound soon made her turn around. Her little friends had not forgotten her. They had been scampering and flying about, as busy as could be, fixing a party dress for her to wear.

"Oh, what a lovely dress!" she cried. "I can't thank you enough," she told all the birds and the mice. She looked out the window. The coach was still there. So she started to dress for the ball.

"Wait!" cried Cinderella to the coachman. "I am coming too!"

She ran down the long stairway just as the stepmother was giving her daughters some last commands. They turned and stared.

"My beads!" cried one stepsister.

"And my ribbon!" cried the other.

"And those bows! You thief! Those are mine!" shrieked the stepmother.

So they pulled and they ripped and they tore at the dress, until Cinderella was in rags once more. And off they flounced.

Poor Cinderella! She ran to the garden behind the house. And there Cinderella sank down on a low stone bench and wept as if her heart would break.

But soon she felt someone beside her. She looked up, and through her tears she saw a sweet-faced woman. "Oh," said Cinderella. "Good evening. Who are you?"

"I am your fairy godmother," said the little woman. And from the thin air she pulled a magic wand. "Now dry your tears. You can't go to the ball looking like that!

"Let's see now, the first thing you will need is — a pumpkin!" said the fairy godmother.

Cinderella did not understand, but she brought the pumpkin.

"And now for the magic words!" The fairy godmother began, "Salaga doola, menchika boola—bibbidi, bobbidi—boo!"

Slowly, up reared the pumpkin on its pumpkin vine, and it turned into a very handsome magic coach.

"What we need next is some fine big— mice!" said the fairy godmother.

Cinderella brought her friends the mice. And at the touch of the wand they turned into prancing horses.

Then Cinderella's old horse became a very fine coachman.

And Bruno the dog turned into a footman at the touch of the magic wand and a "Bib-bidi, bobbidi, boo!"

"There," said the fairy godmother, "now hop in, child. You've no time to waste. The magic only lasts till midnight!"

"But my dress, fairy godmother," said Cinderella as she looked at her rags.

"Good heavens, child!" laughed the fairy godmother. "Of course you can't go in that!"

The wand waved again, and there stood Cinderella in the most beautiful gown in the world, with tiny slippers of glass.

The Prince's ball had started. The palace was blazing with lights. The ballroom gleamed with silks and jewels. And the Prince smiled and bowed, but still looked bored, as all the young ladies of the kingdom in turn curtsied before him.

Up above on a balcony stood the King and the Duke looking on. "Whatever is the matter with the Prince?" cried the King. "He doesn't seem to care for one of those beautiful maidens."

"I feared as much," the Great Grand

Duke said. "He will not fall in love easily."

But just then he did! For at that moment Cinderella appeared at the doorway of the ballroom. The Prince caught sight of her through the crowd. And like one in a dream he walked to her side and offered his arm.

Quickly the King beckoned to the musicians, and they struck up a dreamy waltz. The Prince and Cinderella swirled off in the dance. And the King, chuckling over the success of his plan to find a bride for the Prince, went happily off to bed.

All evening the Prince was at Cinderella's side. They danced every single dance. They ate supper together. And Cinderella had such a wonderful time that she quite forgot the fairy godmother's warning until the clock in the palace tower began to strike midnight.

"Oh, dear!" cried Cinderella. She knew the magic was about to end!

Without a word she ran from the ballroom, down the long palace hall, and out the door. One of her little glass slippers flew off, but she could not stop.

She leaped into her coach, and away they raced for home. But as they rounded the first corner the clock finished its strokes. The spell was broken. And there in the street stood an old horse, a dog, and a ragged girl, staring at a small, ordinary pumpkin.

"Glass slipper!" the mice cried.

And Cinderella looked down. Sure enough, there was a glass slipper on the pavement.

"Oh, thank you, godmother!" she said.

Next morning there was great excitement in the palace. The King was furious when he found that the Great Grand Duke had let the beautiful girl slip away.

"All we could find was this one glass slip-per," the Duke admitted. "And now the Prince says he must marry the girl whom this slipper fits. And no one else."

"He did?" cried the King. "He said he would marry her? Well then, find her!"

All day and all night the Grand Duke with his servant traveled about the kingdom, trying to find a foot on which the glass slipper would fit. In the morning, his coach drove up before Cinderella's house.

The news of the search had spread. The stepmother was busy rousing her daughters and preparing them to greet the Duke. She was determined that one of them should wear the slipper and be the Prince's bride.

"The Prince's bride!" whispered Cinderella. "I must dress, too."

She went off to her room, humming a waltzing tune. Then the stepmother suspected the truth—that Cinderella was the girl the Prince was seeking. So the stepmother followed Cinderella—to lock her in her room.

The mice chattered a warning, but Cinderella did not hear them—she was off in a world of dreams.

Then she heard the key click. The door of her room was locked.

"Please let me out—oh, please!" she cried. But the wicked stepmother only laughed and laughed and went away.

"We will save you!" said the loyal mice. "We will somehow get that key!"

The household was in a flurry. The Great Grand Duke had arrived. His servant held the glass slipper in his hand.

"It is mine!" both stepsisters cried.

And each tried to force her foot into the tiny glass slipper. But the stepsisters failed.

Meanwhile, the mice had made themselves into a long, live chain. The mouse at the end dropped down into the stepmother's dress pocket. He popped up again with the key to Cinderella's room! At once the mice hurried off with the key.

Now the Grand Duke was at the door, about to leave. Suddenly, down the stairs Cinderella came flying.

"Oh, wait, wait, please!" she called. "May I try the slipper on?"

"Of course you may try," said the Great Grand Duke. And he called back the servant with the slipper. But the wicked stepmother tripped the boy. Away sailed the slipper, and crash! it splintered into a thousand pieces. "Oh my, oh my!" said the Duke.

"Never mind," said Cinderella. "I have the other here." And she pulled from her pocket the other glass slipper!

So off to the palace went Cinderella in the King's own coach, with the happy Grand Duke by her side. The Prince was delighted to see her again. And so was his father, the King. For this sweet and beautiful girl won the hearts of all who met her.

In no time at all she was Princess of the land. And she and her husband, the charming Prince, rode to their palace in a golden coach to live

Happily Ever After!

THE SORCERER'S APPRENTICE

THERE WAS ONCE a great sorcerer who knew more about magic than anyone else in the whole world. He lived deep in an underground cavern, alone but for one little apprentice, who was Mickey Mouse.

There was a lot of work to be done in that underground cavern, and Mickey did it all. He did the meal cooking and the floor sweeping and the bed making and errand running and water hauling and wood chopping for the sorcerer. He got very tired of it, too, for it did seem that with all the magic under the sorcerer's tall hat, he should be able to find easier ways of doing the housework.

"If I had that magic hat, I'd never work again!" Mickey thought enviously as he watched the sorcerer weaving magic spells one day. Mickey, at the time, was busy filling the big tub in the middle of the cavern with bucketfuls of water from the well outside. As soon as he rested for a moment to watch the magic, he felt the sorcerer's stern gaze upon him, and he hurried off to fill his buckets. But when he came back again, Mickey found the cavern empty. The sorcerer had gone off to visit a neighboring magician. And he had left his magic hat behind!

This was the moment Mickey had been waiting for. Very cautiously he tip-toed over to the table, picked up the magic hat, and set it on his own head. It fitted perfectly. Being a magic hat, it would fit anyone who wore it, but Mickey did not know that.

"Gee," he thought happily, "I guess probably I was born to be a magician."

Now to test the hat's powers! As Mickey glanced around the gloomy cavern, he spied the old broom leaning against the wall.

"That will do," he thought.

Looking as stern and masterful as he could, Mickey pointed his fingers at the broom.

The broom quivered. Then, while Mickey's eyes grew bigger and rounder with pleased surprise, it jumped away from the wall and began to waddle across the room toward him.

"I'm a sorcerer!" Mickey thought proudly.

"With this magic hat I can do anything my master can. No more housework for me! I'll let the broom do my water carrying!"

"Broom!" he ordered in his sternest tones. "Fill this tub for me!"

The broom bobbed forward in a little nod. Then, as Mickey watched, wide-eyed, it waddled out of the cavern, up the stone steps, to the well, and was soon back with two buckets full of water. Into the tub went the water, and away waddled the broom for more.

This was wonderful. Mickey capered around the room in a gleeful dance, to celebrate his freedom from toil. Then he sank into the sorcerer's armchair and leaned back to dream of all the marvelous things he would do, now that he could make magic.

He smiled with satisfaction at the steady swish of the broom going about its work. Then his head . . . nodded . . . and Mickey . . . dropped off to sleep.

In his dream, Mickey was standing on a great, high cliff overlooking the whole world. Around him the stars and planets wheeled and danced at his every nod and gesture. Far below the ocean roared, and when he beckoned the waves rose up and bowed before him. Higher and higher dashed the

waves, until one broke at his very feet . . . and Mickey awoke with a start.

Water was lapping at his toes. The sorcerer's chair in which he sat was bouncing on a little sea. The whole cavern was flooded! While Mickey slept the broom had worked on, filling the tub to overflowing and finally flooding the whole great room. And here it came now, waddling down the steps to empty two more buckets onto the flood!

"Stop!" cried Mickey. "Stop, broom. Stop, I say!"

He waved his arms. He pointed trembling fingers. He tried every trick and gesture he had seen the sorcerer use, as far as he could

remember, but the broom went sturdily on about its work.

Mickey tried to snatch away the buckets, but still the broom would not be stopped. Then he thought of the ax. With a mighty blow he smashed through the broom's wood handle. Then chop, chop, chop! He hacked it into a hundred bits.

"Well, that's done!" Mickey said to himself with a great sigh as he sank down on

the steps to rest for a moment. "Now to get rid of all this water."

But what was this? Before Mickey's horrified eyes each splinter of wood became a full-sized broom, armed with two water buckets. Now a hundred brooms were hauling water into the cavern which one had filled to flooding!

"No! No! Go back!" he cried, holding out his arms to stop the march of brooms. But on they came, pushing Mickey into the water as they marched with terrible steadiness to the tub, dumped their buckets, then started back to the well.

Poor Mickey! As he floundered in the swirling waters, the sorcerer's book of wisdom floated past, and he snatched at it as his last hope. Pulling it up to a dry step, Mickey began paging through the thick, water-soaked pages in a desperate search for the words that would make everything right again. He was so intent on his search that he did not even notice when a dark shadow fell over the cavern. The sorcerer had returned!

One glance was enough to tell the magic master what had happened.

He lifted his arms in a commanding gesture—and the waters vanished! Mickey could

scarcely believe his eyes, but it was true. The floor of the cavern was dry, the broom leaned lazily against the wall, the tub of water stood waiting, still just half full, with the empty buckets beside it. Everything was just as it had been when the sorcerer had left—all but one small thing. The magic hat was still on Mickey's head.

With a sheepish grin, Mickey handed the hat to the sorcerer. Then without a word he picked up the buckets and raced up the stairs to the well.

"At least," Mickey told himself as he trudged back toward the cavern, a moment later, with the heavy buckets sloshing at his sides, "at least at this job I know how to stop when it's finished!"

THE GRASSHOPPER
AND THE ANTS

"Oh, the world owes me a living,
Tra la la lalala la."

THE grasshopper was singing his song as he jumped through the fields. He almost jumped on top of some ants who were pulling a grain of corn up an ant hill.

Said the grasshopper to the ants:

"Why are you working
All through the day?
A summer day
Is a time to play!"

"We can't play," said the ants. "Winter will soon be here."

The busy little ants did not have time to feel the warm summer sun, or to run and jump just for fun. From the beginning of day till the end, they were busy hauling the corn away. Winter was coming. They had no time to play.

All summer the grasshopper danced his grasshopper dances in the grasses. When he was hungry, he reached out and ate.

And the grasshopper sang:

> *"The good book says:*
> *'The world provides.*
> *There's food on every tree.'*
> *Why should anyone have to work?*
> *Not me!*
> *Oh, the world owes me a living,*
> *Tra la la lalala la."*

With that he took a big swig of honey from a blue harebell that grew above his head. Then he spit a big wet spit of grasshopper tobacco juice. It nearly landed on a little ant who was dragging a load of cherries to store in the ant house for the winter.

Said the grasshopper to the ant:

> *"The other ants can work all day.*
> *Why not try the grasshopper's way?*
> *Come on, let's sing and dance and*
> *play!*
> *Oh, the world owes me a living,*
> *Tra la la lalala la."*

The little ant was so charmed by the music that he dropped his heavy load and started to dance. Then along came the queen, The Queen of All the Ants.

And The Queen of All the Ants frowned on the dancing ant so that he picked up his cherries and went back to the other busy ants. Then The Queen of All the Ants spoke sober words to the grasshopper:

> *"You'll change your tune*
> *When winter comes*
> *And the ground is white with snow."*

The grasshopper made only a courtly bow. "Winter is a long way off," he said. "Do you dance? Let's go."

> *"Oh, the world owes me a living,*
> *Tra la la lalala la.*
> *The other ants can work all day.*
> *Why not try the grasshopper's way?*
> *Come on, let's sing and dance and play!"*

THE GRASSHOPPER AND THE ANTS   219

But even as he sang and danced and played on his fiddle, The Queen of All the Ants hurried away. She, like the other ants, had no time to play.

All through the long lazy summer months the grasshopper went on singing:

"Oh, the world owes me a living,
Tra la la lalala la.
Why are you working
All through the day?
A summer day
Is a time to play!"

There was not tomorrow. There was only today, and the sleet and the snow seemed far away. But the little ants worked harder than ever. As long as the sun was in the sky, they went back and forth carrying the foods from the fields into their ant houses.

Then the winter wind began to blow. It blew the leaves off all the trees. The ants ran into their ant houses and closed the door, and you didn't see them in the fields any more. Every day the winds would blow. And then one day, SNOW.

The grasshopper was freezing. He couldn't find any leaves to eat. All he had was his fiddle and his bow. And he wandered along, lost in the snow. He had nothing to eat and nowhere to go. Then far off he saw one leaf still clinging to a tree.

"Food! Food!" cried the hungry grasshopper, and he leaned against the wind and pushed on toward the tree. But just as he got there the wind blew the last dry leaf away. It fluttered away among the snowflakes. The grasshopper dropped his fiddle and watched the last leaf go. It fluttered away through the white snowflakes. It drifted slowly away. It was gone.

And then the grasshopper came to the house of the busy ants and their Queen. He could hear them inside there having a dance. They had worked hard all summer, and now they could enjoy the winter.

The grasshopper was too cold to go on. The wind blew him over, and he lay there where he fell. His long green jumping and dancing legs were nearly frozen. Then very slowly he pulled himself through the snow to the house of the ants and knocked.

When the ants came to the door, they found him there, half frozen. And ten of the kind and busy ants came out and carried the poor grasshopper into their house. They gave him warm corn soup. And they hurried about, making him warm.

Then The Queen of All the Ants came to him. And the grasshopper was afraid, and he begged of her:

> "Oh, Madam Queen,
> Wisest of ants,
> Please, please,
> Give me another chance."

The Queen of All the Ants looked at the poor, thin, frozen grasshopper as he lay shivering there. Then she spoke these words:

> "With ants, just those
> Who work may stay.
> So take your fiddle—
> And PLAY!"

The grasshopper was so happy that his foot began beating out the time in the old way, and he took up his fiddle and sang:

> "I owe the world a living,
>   Tra la la lalala la.
> I've been a fool
> The whole year long.
> Now, I'm singing
> A different song.
> You were right,
> I was wrong.
>   Tra la la lalala la."

Then all the ants began to dance, even The Queen of All the Ants.

And the grasshopper sang:

> "Now I'm singing
> A different song.
> I owe the world a living,
>   Tra la la lalala la."

THE UGLY DUCKLING

ONE BEAUTIFUL spring morning, a mother duck sat on her nest. Under her, very warm and snug, lay five round eggs. The mother duck was very still, as she sat waiting for her five eggs to hatch.

At last she gave a quack of joy and sprang off the nest. The eggs, in the nest, were moving around and from inside them came the sound of picking and scratching. The mother duck bent her head to watch.

Then one egg shell after another cracked open. Out tumbled one! two! Three! FOUR! ducklings, as yellow as butter, as soft as down, with eyes as bright as black cherries.

With soft little peeps they climbed out of the nest and waddled into the tall grass.

"What a beautiful family!" thought the mother, as she looked at her four ducklings.

But then she looked sadly back at the nest and shook her head. For there lay the fifth and biggest egg, which had not yet hatched. It was a dull, white egg—not at all like the others—but she sat down again and waited.

In a moment a strong bill broke through the shell. Then a head appeared. But the duckling that stumbled out of the egg shell was not small and yellow and downy as its brothers had been. Instead it was big, and white, and clumsy!

"Honk!" said the new duckling, eager to be liked by the mother duck.

"Goodness!" said the mother duck in horror. "This little duckling does not sound like any child of mine."

"Peep!" said the other ducklings. "He's funny looking. We don't want to play with him." And they waddled after their mother down the path to the pond.

The Ugly Duckling couldn't understand why no one would play with him or why they called him ugly. He wanted to be friends, so he followed the others down to the pond.

There was the mother duck swimming in the clear water. On her back sat the four little ducklings having a lovely ride.

"Honk!" called the Ugly Duckling in his friendliest voice, hoping for a ride, too.

But the mother duck just scolded at him and told him to go away.

The poor Ugly Duckling sat alone on the bank of the pond.

"Why won't they play with me?" he wondered sadly. "Why do they call me ugly?" And big tears filled his eyes and dropped into the water below him.

He watched the rings they made as they fell. Suddenly he saw a strange and frightening sight. There, all blurred and twisted with the ripples, was his own reflection!

"Oh dear!" cried the Ugly Duckling. "I am indeed ugly. I will run and hide where no one will have to look at me." So he turned away from the sunny pond and started into the dark forest.

How frightened and lonely he felt there in the deep forest! Silent shadows swayed gloomily beneath the trees as a chilly wind moved their branches to and fro.

Suddenly there was a rush of wings overhead and into the woods flew a whole family of young pheasants.

"Oh," thought the Ugly Duckling, "perhaps they will play with me." And he started towards them hesitantly, hoping that they would not scold him and leave him. But the birds in the bushes flew up as he approached and disappeared between the trees.

"That is because I am so ugly," thought the Ugly Duckling, and he shut his eyes to keep back the tears.

And so it went on the first day, and the second day, and for many days after that.

Once, as he swam alone through the rushes, he met a duck who smiled at him and bobbed pleasantly on the green water.

"At last!" thought the Ugly Duckling happily. "I have found a friend." And he swam up to the new duck and spoke to him timidly. But the new duck only kept smiling and would not answer.

The Ugly Duckling did not guess that his new friend was only a painted toy duck some children had set on the water and allowed to float away.

It was lonely having no one to talk to, but a toy duck was better than none, and so the Ugly Duckling played with him.

But one day, when the water on the pond was ruffled with waves that the wind made, the toy duck turned suddenly with the current and struck the Ugly Duckling sharply on the head with his painted bill.

Weakly the Ugly Duckling swam to shore and rested on the bank. He watched his smiling friend bob off across the water until he was out of sight. He suddenly understood that the little toy duck had no heart at all and therefore could never love him.

The pain in his head was great but the pain in his heart was great still. The Ugly Duckling could no longer keep back his tears and he cried and cried.

Spring turned into summer, summer into fall, and after fall came the cold snows. The Ugly Duckling grew bigger and bigger. During the long winter he had to work hard to stay alive, for food was scarce. Still he was alone and he grew very sad.

Then one day, when the trees around the pond were soft with new green leaves and the forest was alive with spring, something wonderful happened!

The Ugly Duckling was swimming among the rushes at the edge of the pond, when there flew over the water the most beautiful bird he had even seen. After it came another and another. The Ugly Duckling hardly dared to breathe for fear these new creatures would see him and fly away.

"What can they be?" he wondered, enchanted, as he watched them drop on the clear surface. "Surely they are the Kings of Birds, for they are the most beautiful creatures I have ever seen."

Drawn by their grace, hardly realizing what he was doing, the Ugly Duckling swam nearer and nearer.

Suddenly one of the great birds raised its long neck and looked right at him. The Ugly Duckling quickly turned his head to hide. He could not bear to have these beautiful creatures see how ugly he was.

But the great swan (for that was what he was), cried to the others,

"Here's a new one!"

And all the other swans gathered around the Ugly Duckling saying,

"A new one, and the most beautiful of us all!" They bowed their heads before him.

Glancing into the smooth water the Ugly Duckling, or the King of the Swans as we must call him now, saw his own beautiful reflection. How he had changed! His neck had grown curved and graceful, his feathers sleek and white, and his head was marked with handsome black lines. Yes, he was beautiful indeed.

As he floated across the water with his new friends, the mother duck said to her ducklings, "Who is that lovely bird? How beautiful he is!"

The family of pheasants remarked, "How wonderful it would be to be so graceful and so strong!"

Even the little painted duck looked impressed as the swan sailed past.

The Ugly Duckling was very happy now that he had friends, and he kindly forgave the ducks, and the pheasants, and even the little painted duck for the way they had treated him. And as for them—they had learned that you never know when you may meet a King in disguise.

THE BRAVE LITTLE TAILOR

ONCE UPON A TIME there was a little kingdom which was a happy place to live in. It would have kept on being happy but for one thing—a big, enormous giant moved in and went stamping about the countryside, trampling houses and crops under his great boots.

The King himself had offered a reward for the capture of the giant, dead or alive. Everyone wanted him to be captured, but somehow no one knew how to do it. So the giant went on until the whole kingdom was in a terrible state.

Now in the royal city was a little tailor shop. There Mickey Mouse, the tailor, sat and worked all day. The giant did not bother him. What bothered him was flies! Flies swarmed on the ceiling; flies crawled over the table where Mickey sat and sewed; flies zoomed around his nose as he tried to work.

At last, in a great burst of annoyance, Mickey picked up two swatters and slammed them together as a whole swarm of flies went buzzing by. Down fell the victims.

"O boy! Seven at one blow!" Mickey smiled.

Running to the window, he thrust his head out just as one villager passing by said to another, "Did you ever kill a giant?"

"I killed seven at one blow!" cried Mickey, thinking of his swatted flies.

"Seven at one blow!" echoed the villagers, picturing a kingdomful of giants laid out at Mickey's feet.

Mickey nodded happily, and the villagers rushed away to spread the news. Soon the whole town was buzzing with talk of Mickey's great deed.

At last word came to the King himself and his daughter, Princess Minnie.

227

"The little tailor, Your Majesty, killed seven giants with one blow!" panted a guard.

"Seven!" shouted the King. "Bring the tailor here!"

So Mickey Mouse, to his great surprise, found himself being hustled to the palace of the King.

"Did you kill seven at one blow?" thundered the King, as Mickey was brought before the throne.

"Yes, Your Honor. I killed seven," said Mickey, gaining courage from Princess Minnie's smile. "And how!"

"Well," said the King. "How?"

Mickey took a deep breath.

"I was all alone," he explained. "I heard 'em coming. I looked up and I was surrounded. They were here, there, everywhere —a whole bunch of 'em. They came at me from the left, right, left, right—"

The King was hanging on Mickey's every word. "Yes, yes," he encouraged. "Go on!"

"They were coming closer. The fight was on. I swung and missed—I missed and swung. I swung again and again and again. They were right on top of me." Mickey was all excited himself now.

"And then?" said the King.

Mickey drew his long tailor's scissors through the air like a sword.

"Then," he finished proudly, "I let 'em have it!"

"Wow!" said the King. "Brave tailor, I appoint you Royal High Killer of the Giant!"

Mickey's smile faded. He almost collapsed.

"Giant!" he squeaked. "But-but-but-Your Majesty—I-I-I—"

"And your reward," the King continued, "shall be one million pazoozas!"

"Th-thank you, sir," Mickey stammered, "but I-I-I couldn't—"

"Two million pazoozas!" said the King.

"But—I-I-I-I don't know—," Mickey tried to explain.

Now Princess Minnie tugged at her father's sleeve and whispered in his ear.

"Three million pazoozas," smiled the King, "and the hand of the Princess."

"The Princess!" gasped Mickey. "I'll cut that giant right down to my size!"

And away he marched, out of the long throne room, down the palace halls, through the royal city to the great gate in the walls. The streets were filled with cheering people as the hero strode along; banners and handkerchiefs fluttered at windows, and from high in the palace tower, Princess Minnie waved and threw him a kiss.

Mickey Mouse marched along triumphantly to the gates of the city. But as he stood alone on the road outside, and the drawbridge clanked up behind him, he suddenly felt very lonely indeed.

"Gosh," sighed the brave little tailor to himself as he sank down upon a stone. "I don't know how to catch a giant."

As he sat there, with his head in his hands, Mickey felt the rock beneath him tremble, and a great shadow fell across the ground.

"The giant!" Mickey gasped, and he began to run as fast as his legs would carry him.

He ran fast, but the giant's footsteps clomped closer and closer. Soon Mickey came to the shore of a little lake. For a moment he was stopped. But then he spied a rowboat moored near by. Leaping into it, he rowed away at top speed. But his fastest rowing could not save him. The giant splashed into the water behind Mickey, and a great wave from his boot flung the little rowboat up onto the far shore.

Mickey jumped out and raced away, but the huge black shadow of the giant spread across the landscape and the thudding footsteps were very close now. As the giant overtook him, Mickey dove into a cartload of pumpkins and burrowed in among them. He peeked out of his hiding place once, only to see the giant seating himself on a cottage roof beside him. The cottage crumpled softly beneath the tremendous weight, and the

giant grunted a comfortable grunt. Then he spied the load of pumpkins and a hungry smile spread across his face. He reached out and scooped up a great handful of pumpkins —and in the handful was Mickey Mouse!

Mickey scarcely had time to figure out what was happening. He felt himself being lifted through the air. He saw a great dark hole opening before him. It was the giant's mouth, he realized with horror! As the giant flung the pumpkins down his gullet, Mickey managed to catch hold of his great upper lip. From there he swung himself up to the giant's nose. The poor giant twitched uncomfortably, for his nose began to tickle, but as he reached up to rub it, Mickey scrambled to his eyebrow. The giant wrinkled his forehead in a worried frown, and this unexpected motion shook Mickey loose from his hold. Down he plummeted, down through thin air!

"This is the end!" Mickey thought grimly. But with a soft thud he landed unhurt on the giant's palm.

"What a spot!" Mickey groaned.

The giant raised his other palm, ready to squash Mickey flat, but the brave little tailor darted up the giant's big sleeve. As the giant reached in after him, Mickey began sewing, faster than he had ever sewed in his life. Soon the giant's hand was sewed into his sleeve, and as he struggled to free it, Mickey raced up his side, sewing his arms down flat, until the big fellow was completely helpless.

Then Mickey scampered on up until he reached the giant's head, and, still keeping a firm grip on his string, he jumped! Down swung Mickey, whirling round and round the giant's frame until he was completely bound up in the string. Mickey had just jumped to the ground and started to run for all he was worth when the giant, who could not move a muscle, began to topple.

Cr-runch! BANG! The giant crashed down full length to the ground, and the earth quivered and shook for miles around. The giant himself was knocked out completely.

Mickey drew a deep, deep breath, dusted off his hands, and started back to the city and the palace of the King.

What a welcome he received there when the people realized that the giant was in their power! What a celebration there was for the whole countryside! With the giant furnishing wind power, a great, glorious carnival was set up.

Mickey, with millions of pazoozas' reward in the bank, was the hero of the day. But for Mickey, the best reward of all was having the Princess Minnie's hand in his.

So the brave little tailor became prince of the realm, and married his princess and lived happily ever after.

BABES IN TOYLAND

THE GOOD FOLK of Mother Goose Village were excited and delighted. Beautiful Mary Contrary and handsome Tom the Piper were soon to be wed. In the village square, Mother Goose was giving a grand feast for them, and everyone was there.

In all the excitement, no one noticed that Barnaby and his two henchmen were watching from the attic of Barnaby's house.

Wicked Barnaby! He had a secret. Mary did not know it, but soon she would be an heiress. Soon she would be very wealthy. "I must have Mary's money," thought Barnaby.

Then he turned to his henchmen. One was called Gonzorgo, and he was very fat. The other was called Roderigo. He wasn't fat at all. But both were very wicked . . . why, they were almost as wicked as Barnaby.

"If you steal Miss Mary's sheep and then dispose of Tom," the wicked miser told them, "I'll pay you very well. Mary, you see, will think that she is poor. Without Tom, she'll have to marry me!"

As soon as the celebration in the square was over, the two greedy scoundrels set out to do Barnaby's bidding.

They followed when Tom walked Mary home.

They waited while Tom and Mary said good night.

But when Tom started back through Mary's garden gate, they seized him. Quick as a wink they had Tom trussed up in a sack. Then they put him into a wheelbarrow.

"We're on our way to take Tom and throw him in the sea," they sang. "And when the job is finally done, we'll get a handsome fee."

BUMP, BUMP, BUMP went poor Tom in the wheelbarrow as Gonzorgo and Roderigo pushed him along. At last they came to a crossroads. To THE SEA and To GYPSY CAMP, said the signposts.

Gonzorgo had a brilliant idea! "Why not sell Tom to the gypsies?" he said. "Then Barnaby will pay us for taking Tom away, and the gypsies will pay us for giving Tom to them. We'll be paid twice for the same job!"

Roderigo agreed. And off they went to the gypsy camp.

Early the next morning, Gonzorgo and Roderigo hurried to Mary's house. Barnaby was already there. The wicked wretch said he had come to wish Tom and Mary happiness.

Pretending to be sailors, Gonzorgo and Roderigo told Mary a sad tale. "Tom was at sea with us last night when a sudden storm came up. Alas," lamented Gonzorgo, "it washed him overboard."

Mary was stunned. "But why did Tom run off to sea?"

"He was poor," explained Gonzorgo. "Unable to support you, he ran away to set you free. Now you can marry wealthy Barnaby."

"That's an excellent suggestion," said the sly Barnaby.

Kindly, but firmly, Mary refused Barnaby. She did not want wealth. The sheep had always given her family a livelihood.

At that moment Bo Peep appeared, tears streaming down her pretty face. "I have lost the sheep!" she cried. "What will we do?"

Gonzorgo and Roderigo had successfully carried out the other part of Barnaby's evil scheme!

"Never mind, Bo Peep," soothed Mary. "You'll find them again."

"But they went into the Forest of No Return!" Bo Peep sobbed.

"How horrible!" cried Mary.

Barnaby smirked. "How will you and your brothers and sisters get along now? Perhaps

you should consider my offer again." And he took himself off to his crooked house, leaving Mary in great distress.

Indeed, how would Mary get on now? Without the sheep, she had no income at all! She tucked her little brothers and sisters into bed that night, assuring them that all would be well. But Mary herself was not so sure, and the children knew it.

Later, from their bedroom window, they watched Mary walk into the garden. She stopped and looked at Barnaby's crooked house, where a single dim light burned in the attic window. Then, very slowly, Mary began to walk toward that evil, beckoning light.

"She's going to marry Barnaby!" said one of the children.

"We must stop her!" said another.

"If we could find the sheep, she wouldn't have to marry him," suggested a third, feeling very brave. "Come on. Let's go!"

CLING! CLANG! CLING! Wildly, Gonzorgo and Roderigo rang the town bell. "Wake up, everybody! Wake up!" they shouted. CLING! CLANG! CLING! "Good news! Good news!"

The sleepy townspeople tumbled out of bed and ran to the square. There was Barna-by, smiling his crooked smile. And there was poor Mary, sad and pale, her hand caught fast in Barnaby's damp grip.

The good people of Mother Goose Village were shocked and silent when Barnaby announced his news. He and Mary were to be married!

"Don't grieve for Tom," she said, peering at Mary's palm. "He's alive!" Suddenly the gypsy threw off her tatters. It was Tom in disguise! Mary rushed into his arms and cried with happiness.

Barnaby was furious! Quickly, he ran off in search of the double-crossers. No more mistakes would be made. He would see to that!

Suddenly a band of gypsies burst into the square and began to sing and dance. Barnaby had hired them to help celebrate his betrothal.

Gonzorgo and Roderigo stared at them in horror. These were the same gypsies who had bought Tom! Terrified, they hid. Would Barnaby discover their deception?

The dancing was at its wildest when an old gypsy fortune teller came forth and beckoned to Mary.

Together, the happy couple walked to Mary's house. But bad news awaited them. Pinned to the door was a note from the children.

"Dear Sweet Mary," it said, "please don't marry Barnaby. We have gone to the Forest of No Return to find our lost sheep."

Horrified, Tom and Mary set out after the children. In their haste, they didn't notice the three silent shadows that followed them into the gloomy, forbidding forest.

Through the lonely, sighing woods, Tom and Mary searched. The night was at its blackest when at last they found the children, huddled together in a clearing.

The children were overjoyed to see their rescuers, and to know that Tom was still alive. "We're so happy to see you!" they cried. "We've been so afraid. The trees in this awful forest move and speak! They told us we could never leave here!"

"Now, now," Mary soothed. "It was only your imagination."

"Let's stay here until daybreak," suggested Tom. "When it is light enough, we'll find the sheep and then go home. You'll see."

Mary gathered the children to her and crooned a lullaby. Before long, the children's heads were nodding. Even Tom was asleep.

Only Barnaby and his henchmen, hidden behind some bushes, watched through the night.

The next morning, Tom and Mary awoke to find themselves surrounded by trees. They really did move. And they really did speak.

"This is the Forest of No Return," a tall pine told Tom. "Those who stumble in, those who fumble in, never can get out! The Toymaker in Toyland must decide your fate."

Suddenly the children forgot their fear. The very thought of seeing Toyland delighted them. "We're really going to go there?" they asked the trees. "You won't change your minds, will you?"

"Of course not! Line up right now!" directed an oak.

The trees marched Tom and Mary and the children off to Toyland. Along the way they all sang, loud and clear.

"Toyland! Toyland! Dear little girl and boy land.
While you dwell within it, you are ever happy then.
Childhood's Toyland, wonderful world of joy land.
Once you leave its borders, you can never return again."

Suddenly, there before them was Toyland! The children had never seen anything so wonderful! Fantastic toy figures and a hundred weather vanes covered the big white house that stood in the center of an island.

Tom led the children across the bridge, past the toy sentries that guarded the open gates, and up to the door of the Toy Factory.

There they saw a sign: CLOSED FOR ALTERATIONS. Although no one answered his knock, Tom heard voices coming from inside.

The voices belonged to the Toymaker and Grumio, his assistant. Grumio had just invented a toy-making machine, and he was showing the Toymaker how it worked.

"You push a button for the things you want. For a girl doll, push Sugar, Spice, Everything Nice, and Golden Hair," Grumio explained. He demonstrated by punching the buttons himself.

The machine began snorting and chuffing. Motors turned, pistons and arms whirled, and lights flashed. Sweet music filled the air —and a little Dutch doll dropped out.

"But," Grumio cautioned the Toymaker, "it's a very delicate machine. You must be careful not to overload it."

The Toymaker, eager to test the invention, didn't hear Grumio's advice. He pushed buttons for Boat . . . Block . . . Train . . . Airplane . . . Toy Soldier. . . .

Whistles screeched, rockets went off, and a neon sign flashed. The Toymaker had overloaded the machine! The arms and pistons flew off in a great explosion.

When the smoke had cleared away, all that was left of the machine was dust.

"Oh, dear!" said the Toymaker, picking himself up and brushing the dust from his coat. "It's half past October, and no toys are ready yet. It may be a very sad Christmas."

At that moment, Tom stepped forward and introduced himself. He said that if the children could help with the toys, the Toymaker might have the presents ready in time after all.

The Toymaker agreed, and soon the children were working on an assembly line. They painted smiles on the dolls' faces and wrapped the other toys in big gay packages.

In the evening, Tom and Mary tucked the little workers into makeshift beds in the storeroom. As they all went to sleep, evil Barnaby lurked nearby, waiting to kidnap Mary.

After everyone was deep in slumber, Grumio burst in on the Toymaker! He had invented a special formula that would reduce an object to the size of a toy.

Overjoyed, the Toymaker filled a spray gun with the formula and aimed it at his bed. POOF! A toy-sized bed! POOF! A chair turned into a miniature chair! POOF! POOF! POOF! The Toymaker poofed everything in sight.

Standing in the room full of toys, the Toymaker said, "Grumio, you're a genius!"

Then the Toymaker became unhappy. "Where am I going to get enough big things to make into small things?" he wondered. Then he turned to Grumio. "This thing is no help to me at all, Grumio. You and your silly inventions!"

Discouraged and unhappy, the Toymaker threw Grumio's poof-gun out the bedroom window.

Standing just outside was Barnaby, who picked up the gun with a nasty chuckle. It would help him to carry out his evil scheme.

The first thing Barnaby did was point the gun at the Toymaker. POOF! The Toymaker was toy-size!

Gonzorgo and Roderigo were shocked. Realizing that Barnaby intended to use the gun on everyone, they had a change of heart. "We want nothing more to do with this horrible plot," they told him.

"Then I will turn the poof-gun on you!" replied Barnaby.

Barnaby pointed the gun at his former friends.

Gonzorgo and Roderigo hid behind a huge barrel. POOF! The barrel was toy-size, and they loomed like giants behind it.

Then Barnaby took aim once more. POOF! The formula hit Roderigo! POOF! The formula hit Gonzorgo! Barnaby picked up the two fleeing men between his thumb and forefinger and deposited them in a bird cage.

Next on Barnaby's list was Tom. POOF! In the wink of an eye, Tom became only six inches high!

Then Barnaby found his way to Mary. He hovered over her like a big black bird. Frightened, Mary screamed for Tom.

Laughing an evil laugh, Barnaby plucked Tom out of his pocket and set him down near the bird cage. Poor Tom! He was all tied up with red ribbon. Barnaby turned to Mary with a sneer. "Now I will have your hand in marriage!" he commanded.

"Never!" sobbed Mary. "Never!"

"Oh, yes!" countered Barnaby. "May I remind you that one more shot of this formula will make Tom disappear—forever!"

Mary had no choice. "The marriage will take place immediately!" said Barnaby. "The Toymaker will marry us."

When the ceremony started, Tom inched closer to the cage. It was a simple matter for Gonzorgo to untie Tom's bonds.

Free once more, Tom jumped to a chair and then to the floor. He slipped through a crack in the door and ran into the shipping room. First he cut the ribbons on all the boxes. Then he blew a call to arms on a toy trumpet.

Row on row of toy soldiers fell into line. Battleships and cannons, Trojans and Indians —all answered the call.

Tom and his toy army arrived in the workshop just as Barnaby and Mary were about to be pronounced man and wife.

"Stop!" shouted Tom. Telling Mary to take cover, he jumped on his hobby horse and led the troops into battle.

The battleship fired, filling Barnaby's mouth with marbles.

The Indians unloosed their arrows, and the suction cups stuck to Barnaby's nose.

But Barnaby fought back. With his foot, he swept the whole army off its wooden feet. He hurled a battleship into a pail of water, and its toy admiral sank to the bottom. Reaching for the toy soldiers, he hurled them against the wall.

"Enough of this horse play," Barnaby muttered, and he pulled out the poof-gun. He planned to reduce everything to oblivion.

Then a zeppelin flew over, and dropped its load of marbles.

The marbles proved to be Barnaby's undoing. While the wicked fellow was slipping and sliding on them, Mary picked up a discarded toy gunboat and put a marble in its cannon.

POW! The marble met its mark. It shattered the poof-gun, and the liquid spattered all over Barnaby.

Now that Barnaby was toy-size, Tom attacked once more. Tom, with his sword, and Barnaby, with his crooked cane, fought back and forth over the littered floor of the Toy Factory. They parried and thrust for many long minutes, but Tom's skill with the sword finally overcame Barnaby's sly tricks.

Tom maneuvered Barnaby toward an open box. One quick lunge and—BOOM!—Barnaby fell backward, right into the box. Tom leaped forward and shut the lid. At last, Barnaby was a prisoner!

The soldiers all cheered Tom's victory. The toys would never forget what he had done.

No sooner was the battle over than Grumio ran into the room. He had another new invention—a magic restoring formula.

"This is just what we need!" said the Toymaker. "I'm sorry I scolded you before, Grumio," he went on. "Please forgive me."

Grumio sprayed the new formula all around the room, restoring the toy furniture to its full size.

He sprayed it on the Toymaker and Tom, who returned to their regular height.

Then he unlocked the bird cage and freed Gonzorgo and Roderigo. He sprayed them, too.

Grumio sprayed all the wounded and broken soldiers, and they became as good as new. Their red coats were as bright as ever, and their guns were straight again. The toy admiral was hale and hearty—and dry!

He sprayed it on everybody—except Barnaby, who was still safely inside the box.

In fact, Grumio's new formula made it possible for all the toys to be ready in time for Christmas. And the Toymaker was so happy that he pinned a great big Hero Medal on Grumio's chest.

A few days later, back in Mother Goose Village, there was another celebration. It was in honor of Tom and Mary's wedding.

Mother Goose held the Toymaker's bird cage in her hand, and inside the cage was Barnaby. He was still toy-size—and that's the way they intended to keep him.

And so Tom and Mary were married, and lived happily ever after . . . with the Babes in Toyland.

Mary's House

Mother Goose Village

Forest of No Return

Barnaby's House

Toyland